The Fightback

The Wrong Side of the Tracks, Volume 3

Lexy Timms

Published by Dark Shadow Publishing, 2022.

THE FIGHTBACK

First edition. August 5, 2022.

Written by Lexy Timms.

THE FIGHTBACK

By LEXY TIMMS

THE WRONG SIDE OF THE TRACKS #3
THE
FIGHTBACK
USA TODAY BESTSELLING AUTHOR
LEXY TIMMS

The Fightback

The Wrong Side of the Tracks Series #3

Cover by: Book Cover by Design[1]

1. **http://bookcoverbydesign.co.uk/**

The Wrong Side of the Tracks

The Knockback
The Overshare
The Fightback

Find Lexy Timms:

Lexy Timms Newsletter:
http://www.lexytimms.com/newsletter
Lexy Timms Facebook Page:
https://www.facebook.com/LexyTimmsAuthor
Lexy Timms Website:
http://www.lexytimms.com

Want to read more...
For **FREE**?
Sign up for Lexy Timms' newsletter
And she'll send you updates on new releases, ARC copies of books
and a whole lotta fun!
Sign up for news and updates!
http://www.lexytimms.com/newsletter

The Fightback

SOMETIMES IN LIFE, you must fight back...

When Gavin and Lila last saw each other, she'd run after a passionate embrace on the beach. Gavin's injury and the distraction of the Lila-Star situation ends with him having a poor showing during the tournament, while Lila uses it to fuel her into becoming a superstar overnight.

When they get back home, Lila and Star finally talk and Star completely acts like the breakup with Gavin is no big deal, but doesn't seem to be acting the same way. Meanwhile, Gavin is happy for his roommate and best friend Kevin for falling into a relationship with Lila's friend Emma, and is trying to clear the air with Star so he can pursue Lila.

When Lila and Gavin finally meet again, things get explosive, but despite what Star is saying, is she really okay with the new relationship? And when the fight and ransom payment to the gang comes back to haunt Gavin, will he be able to salvage his career before scandal takes him down for the sin of saving his families lives?

Will Lila and Gavin be able to finally be happy together, or are the star-crossed lovers doomed to never be one?

THE WRONG SIDE OF THE TRACKS #3

THE FIGHTBACK

USA TODAY BESTSELLING AUTHOR

LEXY TIMMS

Chapter One

Lila

"NO, YOU CAN'T GO HOME," Emma pleaded. "We just won! You're a star! You have to stay and party with us!"

"I don't know, Emma," I grumbled. "I'm tired. I just want to be in my own bed at home. Plus, there's this whole thing with Star, and..."

"She won't be home yet either, come on! Come party with us girls. It's just us. All the boys are going home."

She had a point. It wasn't like I would be subjecting myself to seeing Gavin anymore, and I hadn't really hung out with the girls at all. Even the little bit of time I had seen them, I had been starry-eyed about Gavin, and Emma had been busy with her tryst with Kevin, a situation that was looking a lot more serious than I initially thought it would be. Especially considering the reputation both of them had of not being serious with anyone and playing both fields rather extensively.

Plus, getting an Uber to get home was going to be expensive. An expense I probably couldn't afford, especially considering the bus home had been pushed back for us.

"Let me think about it," I said. "I haven't even gotten out of my uniform yet."

"Fine," Emma said, shrugging and padding down the hall a few feet, "but I will be back in a half hour. I better find you wearing something sexier than jeans, girl."

"I'll think about it," I repeated and shut the door between us.

Finally, it was quiet, only the sound of the air conditioner blowing in the background. I sighed, turning toward the empty room and trying to decide what to do. I really was exhausted. I had played my ass off, and like Emma said, made myself a star during it. In three starts, I went eighteen innings, throwing twenty strikeouts and only allowing one run, and that was off an error. On top of that, I had a game-winning home run in the second game and hit well all weekend. I was dominant.

It was the best I had ever played, and yet the worst I had ever felt.

There was so much going on in my head, my body was worn completely down, and all I wanted to do was sit in a hot bathtub and go to sleep. Yet, at the same time, being alone had absolutely zero enticing factors to it as well, and at least I wouldn't have to see Gavin. Not after the night at the beach. Not after I walked away from him.

I felt a little guilty for how the boys played after that. Gavin clearly felt he had something to prove and had gone out there with the intention of giving everything he had. Which he did. Unfortunately, with his injury, that wasn't a whole lot.

Not watching them play was a choice that seemed to alert some of the girls that there was something wrong with me, but with the way I played, none of them said anything except for Emma. She came to ask about me after the boys' first game, dropping by my room rather than going to see Kevin. I tried to brush it off as being tired, but I could tell she knew something was up.

At any rate, she gave me the run-down of the games. Beaten in the last game of the series, they were knocked out in a pretty humiliating fashion. Gavin, the star of the entire tournament, only made it through one inning as a pitcher, mysteriously pulled from the game after letting up one run and striking out two. The rumor had been there was a shoulder injury.

I knew what the real score was. The shoulder was certainly part of it. But there was so much more.

It was a far cry from my performance. Three starts as a pitcher and batting over four hundred, I looked like an Olympian out there. Or so said Coach. Secretly I wondered if I would have played as well if I weren't taking out all my frustrations on the ball.

The school had sent Coach a message that they wanted to reward the team for its performance and were offering to pay for an extra day for all of us to stay at the hotel. It meant not getting home until Tuesday afternoon, but only a few of us would miss more than two classes and the allure of hanging out on the beach on a Monday, after most of the tourists would have gone home, was too much for them to say no to. The boys were not invited.

I crossed my room to the bathroom and disrobed, absolutely meaning to draw a bath and sit there until Emma came pounding on the door. Relaxing a bit would be nice, and my muscles would thank me after such a hard weekend of wearing myself out. But as I got undressed, I could hear girls in the hall, giggling and laughing. Enjoying themselves in celebration.

And none of them deserved to celebrate their performance any more than I did.

I was being silly. I was being a bad teammate too.

Once I got the water running, I switched it to a shower, hopped in, and got myself clean before I could really relax at all. If I let myself relax too much, I wouldn't want to leave.

Getting out, I grabbed my phone to see two notifications. One was an email, and the other a text from Emma. It was a picture of her wearing what I assumed counted as a dress but looked a little bit more like someone had simply wrapped her body in about four inches of spandex. The message above it simply asked, 'Think this will make Kevin jealous?'

I sent back a thumbs-up. I wasn't getting involved in whatever silly games those two had going on.

Still nothing else from Star, though. She had only sent a one-word message, 'ok', since I laid everything out and told her what had happened. It meant that when I did get home, and Star showed up too, life was going to be a little bit unpredictable. I honestly didn't know how she was going to react. The closest thing to a fight Star and I ever had was over what kind of pizza to order or which TV show to get caught up on first. I had long since given up hope she could do dishes or put things away properly, and she had long given up the idea that I was going to appreciate art the same way she did.

But she was my best friend. My roommate. I didn't want to ruin things with her, and yet, I felt like I already had. I had a sense of doom about going home because I knew it meant having to face her and my actions. And hers. It wasn't like she was totally innocent here.

I got dressed just before Emma started banging on the door, and though she looked at me like I disappointed her when she saw what I was wearing, she tried to be chipper and grabbed my arm to guide me out of the hotel room.

Thankfully, the nightclub we had gone to with Gavin and Kevin wasn't the destination. Instead, one of the girls who came from a wealthier family had rented a limo. It was taking two trips to a club a little farther down the strip, picking up half of us the first go round and the rest on the second. Which left Emma and me standing outside waiting for it to get back to us.

"I'm going to need you to not be a frown-face all night," Emma said as we huddled with the group of girls and tried to avoid the catcalls of other boys walking by.

"I'm trying," I said.

"Good," she said. "No boys tonight. Just us girls."

"Uh huh," I said. "Except you like girls. And you are having fun teasing Kevin."

"Both of those things are true," she said, "but tonight isn't about hooking up, either. It's about celebrating. You specifically. You kicked ass this weekend, Lila."

"Yeah, yeah," I said. "I know."

"Yeah, yeah?" she mocked, turning to a few of the other girls on the team and getting their attention. "Lila is acting like this weekend was no big thing."

"Girl, you better put some respect on your own name," Tamara said. "You made them bitches look silly."

"Silly," Emma agreed.

"What, like, twenty Ks? And a walk-off?" Tamara continued.

"Someone needs to buy her drinks," Saraya said from the crowd. She was always instigating the alcohol aspect of any get-together. "I vote moneybags McKinze."

"Is she the one paying for the limo?" Emma asked. "I thought it was Stacy."

"Who cares? Both of their folks are loaded. McKinze bought an iPhone yesterday because she thought she lost hers the night before. It was under her bed," Tamara laughed.

"Just bought it outright?" Emma asked.

"Put it on Daddy's card," Tamara said. "Dropped a grand and a half like nothing."

"Yeah, she can afford drinks," Saraya said.

"I would think so," Tamara said.

"It depends on how much Saraya puts down," Emma joked.

"I'll be good!" Saraya laughed.

"Or good at it," Tamara muttered.

"Shit, he's here," Emma said, then turned to me. "Dance. Dance and drink and dance some more. Fuck all this drama. Let's have fun, okay? We can worry about drama on the bus."

I nodded and took a deep breath. Just dance. I could do that.

The next morning was a slow one, most of the girls nursing various stages of hangovers. Thankfully, being the Monday after Spring Break, the hotel was mostly empty, and there wasn't a bunch of noise to wake us up. Emma ended up in my room, passed out on the couch, half clothed. I had been almost completely sober when I got back, finding that the more I drank, the more I thought about Gavin.

But by the time I got out of bed and washed off the makeup from the night before, Emma was up, standing in the middle of my room and looking around confused.

"Oh, thank goodness," she said. "I thought I ended up in a stranger's room last night."

"You don't remember coming back to my room with me?" I chuckled. "You kept asking if Gavin and Kevin were going to be here and didn't listen when I told you they were in their own rooms."

"I have zero recollection of that," she said. "Anyway, I see some of our girls are out on the beach. You want to come get some sun with me?"

"I don't know," I said. "I don't feel great about my bikini..."

"Hush," she said. "You're a knockout. Gavin certainly thought so, didn't he?"

I froze. I hadn't said anything to her specifically about what was going on with Gavin and me. As far as she knew, we were just friends, and Gavin was still with Star. But it wasn't like she was blind either. I guessed we weren't as smooth at this as we thought we were.

"Look," she continued, "it's just going to be us out there. The boys are catching the bus in like twenty minutes. We will have a fruity cocktail or something to get a hair of the dog, and then we'll swim and get some sun. Just a relaxing day at the beach. You earned that."

"Sure," I said. "Yeah, all right."

"Meet you at my room when you're ready," she said. "I'll wait for you."

"Okay."

Emma took off, a little wobbly still, and left my room. I pulled out the bikini that I had never really intended on wearing in front of people, thinking I might only wear it for some night-time swimming if possible, and sighed. Once I had it on, I stared in the mirror for a moment.

Gavin had seemed to like this body. It wasn't like I was grotesque or anything, just... large. Solid. An athlete's body. And not one of those volleyball girls. I was built for power.

Emma, on the other hand, was built like a well-endowed fairy. It made her a decent speed threat on the basepaths, since no one expected her, and her strike zone was very tight. But when I saw her in the hallway, I had to roll my eyes. Her bikini, despite the laws of decency, barely covered more of her skin than the dress she'd worn the night before. The first wave that hit her was going to pop a titty out.

Maybe that was the point. She'd probably record it and send it to Kevin.

I spent the day sunning myself, relaxing on the sand and sipping fruit drinks. It was nice, but my mind kept going back to the beach at night, just past the dunes, and Gavin. How he'd held me. How he'd kissed me. How hard his body had been underneath mine.

How much I had wanted him right then. Needed him. And denied myself.

I did the right thing. I had to remember that. I did the right thing.

The boys apparently had gotten stranded with a bus breaking down, but I didn't see any of them all night. I was sure Emma ended up with Kevin at some point, but Gavin never tried to contact me, nor did I see him on the beach or anywhere else. I couldn't tell if I was disappointed by that or not.

That night, my dreams were fitful, and when I got up the next morning to catch the bus back to Georgia, I was groggy and tired. And I couldn't think about anything other than Gavin, Star, and the drama that awaited me at home.

Thankfully, the bus ride was smooth, and I slept through most of it until I got home. The apartment was still dark when I got there, and I slipped inside, went directly to the bathroom, and started the shower. Lunch had been served on the bus, and dinner could wait. I just wanted to wash the week off me as soon as possible.

Chapter Two

Gavin

I WAS MISERABLE. ABSOLUTELY miserable.

The last game had pushed me right past my limit, and I kept going anyway. The black eye I could explain away. I was an athlete on Spring Break. The idea I might have had a few too many drinks, fell and hit my face on something was an easy sell. Coach bought it, though he wasn't happy with me. But everything else was no good.

Playing designated hitter wasn't exactly my favorite thing, but I lucked out in that Coach had already penciled me for that before, seeing I wasn't in great shape. I probably could have handled duties out in center field, where I played when I wasn't pitching, but being able to chill on the bench and only take swings was better for me in my condition.

Still, my performance wasn't great. It wasn't terrible, but not great either. I banged a double in my first at bat that should have been a triple, but I just didn't have the strength in my legs. Then I went hitless the rest of the game, striking out twice. Coach chalked it up to their lefty relievers and an inconsistent strike zone from the ump, but I knew better. I just couldn't follow the ball to the bat and was overthinking every time I got in the box.

The second game was better, going two for five, a double and a single. Three RBIs, so that was good. But still, two more strikeouts. I wasn't used to that as a hitter. Again, Coach complained about the zone, but he was clearly noticing something was up. I knew I wasn't moving right but was trying to mask it. In the seventh, I got moved to the mound, and ended up throwing two innings of relief. The fastball was lively, and I saw the speed gun hit ninety-seven. My slider was on point too, moving across the plate on a dip, moving down and away from righties and disappearing before their bats got through the zone. The first of those two innings I got out of there on eight pitches. It looked like I was ready to start the next game.

Then I took the mound. It was the last game of the tournament for us. The semi-final of the tournament we were heavily favored to win. I was going to the mound as the starter, knowing I was supposed to go five innings and then move to center field. No DH because of my spot on the mound. It was a calculated risk we took every time I pitched, and one that had only seen us lose once doing it in regular season games.

Never, not in any game from Little League on, had I sucked as hard as I did in that semi-final pitching performance.

The warm-up was fine. I was distracted, but it was fine. The girls were on the other field, in the process of destroying their opponents en route to the tournament final. I caught glimpses of Lila on the mound that night, and she looked incredible. Then it would bring up everything about the night on the beach, and I would get a pall over me. I felt stupid and weak. I was sailing balls over the catcher's head.

He said something to Coach before I even took the mound, and when the first pitch I threw bounced in the dirt in front of home plate, I thought I was going to get yanked right then. But the next pitch was a good slider, then a curve, then a one-two four seam fastball, high and tight. Strike three.

I felt like I might be okay.

Then three straight hits. A fielder's choice out that scored the third run. A long fly ball deep into right center that resulted in a double off the wall. Then two walks. I pitched out of the jam by luck, inducing a ground ball up the middle that our shortstop just got a glove on and was able to flip to second to get the force.

Coach pulled me as soon as I got to the dugout and asked if I was all right. I shook my head. My arm was dead. It felt like I had filled it with molten lava. Coach nodded, told me to go get a shower, and I was done.

By the time I got back to the dugout, ice on my shoulder and the team physical therapist peppering me with questions, we were down six to two. We ended up losing seven to three.

All I could think was how I had just let everyone down. I let down my teammates. I let down Kevin. I let down Coach. I let down Star. I let down Lila. I let down *myself.*

This had been the worst week of my life, and as we walked back to the hotel, most of the guys stayed to watch the girls. They had one more game that night. I couldn't make myself do it. Kevin stayed, but I went back to my room and packed. The bus was going to leave tomorrow, and I just wanted to get on, put in earphones and zone out until I got home.

That was not meant to be either.

I overslept, having forgotten what time to set the alarm for, and woke up to Kevin knocking on my door asking if I was okay. Thankfully, I had packed the night before, but I didn't get my chance to eat breakfast or get to the bus first or anything. By the time I boarded, I was just happy to get a spot next to Kevin.

The bus had gotten about six feet before it stopped abruptly. Fifteen minutes later, we were shuffled off the bus and back to the hotel. The bus had broken down.

The girls were staying another day, and many of them were already out on the beach. I didn't see Lila out there, but apparently Kevin had gotten a text with a picture of Emma. Despite my best efforts to avoid it, he showed me anyway. It was certainly a bikini. Not much of one. But a bikini.

It got me thinking about what Lila would wear. My stomach clenched. I needed to stop that.

That ship had sailed.

It was hard not to think about it all the time. I had been so close. My hands had been wrapped around her, her body grinding on mine. My cock felt like it was going to burst out of my shorts when it felt her warmth above it. Our lips had been pressed into each other, and I could taste her. It was exquisite, and being on the beach, in the middle of the night, the stars above us twinkling in the black night... it was perfect.

Then she walked away.

It stuck in my mind, and I played it over and over again.

We ended up staying the night an extra night, but under strict orders from Coach not to go anywhere. While they were paying for an extra night much like they had for the girls, our bus was going to be leaving at six in the morning, well before theirs at twelve. We had to be up early.

Grumbling, we all went back to our rooms, some going for a swim down at the beach but most of us hanging out in our rooms and winding down after a rough weekend. I locked myself in my room and tried to ignore any noise next door when Emma found out Kevin was going to be there an extra night.

Then morning came, and I was standing outside before daybreak, watching the sun rise over the ocean and feeling like absolute crap. Finally, I was boarding a new bus, a considerably smaller one, crammed up against the window with Kevin beside me. Kevin tried to take up as little space as he could, but being almost seven foot tall, it was a hard thing to do. So I scrunched, putting my hoodie under my head and flipping the hood itself over my eyes to block the night. I wanted to sleep.

Then I realized fifteen minutes into the drive, still in Myrtle Beach, no less, that my wireless earbuds were dead.

I hadn't charged the case all week. They were useless. Which left me to sit beside Kevin and listen to his phone have notification after notification after notification. I could see from my vantage point what they were most of the time. I couldn't help it, each ding made me open my eyes.

Some of them were texts, which thankfully I couldn't read. I didn't want to know what they were saying to each other. But others were pictures, the sea prominent in some, Emma's barely-held-together chest in others. She was sending him an average of a message every ten minutes and a picture every thirty. The girls must have gotten up early to get one last shot at the ocean before their bus came.

Six hours into the ride back to Georgia, early-afternoon heat and the dozens of bodies making the bus insufferable to breathe in, and Kevin fell asleep. Thankfully, he had put the phone on mute or Do Not Disturb first, and it afforded me the chance to get a little bit of rest.

I looked at my phone as we neared the Georgia state line. Star hadn't sent anything. I didn't know if that was a good thing or a bad thing. It was possible she had just cut me off, and that was that. Considering I didn't think Lila was going to want anything to do with me anymore, and maybe that was for the best. I wouldn't speak to either one of them ever again.

Or she was just waiting for me to get back to Georgia. That was a possibility too. She could want to lay into me when I got there, giving me all the reasons I was a terrible person. I had a bunch of ammunition to defend myself, but why bother? What was the point? She would never see what she did as anything remotely as bad as what I was sure she thought had happened with me and Lila.

Not that knowing the exact mechanics of the truth would make it any better.

As the bus rattled into Georgia, I checked my phone one last time. Still nothing. Nothing from Star. Nothing from Lila. I frowned and felt relief at the same time. When the bus stopped near the campus, I elbowed Kevin awake, and we grabbed our stuff. He was checking his phone as he got off the bus and grinned.

"Hey boss, you good alone tonight?" he asked.

"Yeah, what's up?"

"Emma's bus should be getting here in a few hours, and she wanted to see if I wanted to get dinner when she got in. I was thinking of dropping my stuff off, grabbing a shower, and getting a reservation somewhere."

"Sure," I said. "Sounds good."

"You sure, bud?" he asked.

"I'll be fine," I said. "Long weekend. It'll be nice to have a few hours alone at home, actually. Just to decompress."

"Word," he said. "All right, let's get this shit home then."

We walked back to the apartment, and he dropped off his stuff in his room without bothering to unpack. I heard him hop in the shower and his electric razor going almost immediately, and when the door opened to the bathroom, it came with a waft of cologne and hair gel.

"Beard looks good," I said as I passed him on the way to the kitchen.

"Thanks, boss." He beamed. "Think Emma will like it?"

"I'm sure she will," I said, pouring myself a glass of water. I felt dehydrated. It was like the bus had sapped me of all my fluids.

"All right. Don't wait up," he said, grabbing his wallet and keys.

"Be safe," I said. "Have fun."

As the door shut, I smiled. It was good seeing Kevin excited about someone. He deserved that.

Unlike me.

I stood in the kitchen and finished my water, wondering if I would ever hear from either one of them, or if the worst weekend of my life had taken everyone out of it except Kevin. Maybe my career too.

Chapter Three

Lila

THERE WAS SOMETHING to be said for having your own towels.

Hotel towels were nice and all, but in the back of my mind, I couldn't quite forget that hundreds of other people had used them. No matter how thoroughly they were washed, it still kind of bugged me. But my own towels, well, those were mine. Star had her own towels, and unlike everything else in the house that became communal the second she and I were living together, towels were something she was particular about. Something about the fabric of some of them made her brain go all fizzy. Or so she said.

So my towels were my own. Only mine. They smelled like my brand of cleaner, and I was safe in the knowledge that only one of them had ever been used for anything other than drying myself after a shower, and that was to help clean up from the one and only time I decided it would be nice to eat and have a glass of wine in bed.

Piling a couple towels up and going through my drawer to find the comfiest pair of sweatpants and the absolute frumpiest T-shirt I could manage to go under the hoodie I planned on wearing to bed, I was just about ready for my shower. I wanted maximum comfort tonight. Something to get my mind off the week's drama and to chill me out before the drama that was surely to come.

Running the water as hot as I could stand it, I decided to go ahead and step in when my phone rang. I sighed and shut the faucet off when

I saw the name on the screen. I could ignore a lot of people, but my mother was not one of them. She was the type of woman to keep calling until I picked up and berate me once I did for wasting her time.

"Hi, Mom," I said when I answered the phone, shoving on the bathrobe I kept by the door back.

"Lila, it's about time I heard from you," Mom said in the tones of a woman who needed to establish who had the power in a conversation immediately.

"Sorry Mom, I've been busy," I said. "We had a tournament out of town in Myrtle Beach, remember? I told you I was going to be starting a couple games, and you said that it was convenient since the family owns a house out there?"

"No, dear, I don't," she said. "I presume it went well? Not abandoning sports for something using your mind yet?"

"It went great, actually," I said with enough sass in my voice to get a backhand if I had been face to face. "I was the star of the tournament, and we won."

"Oh, lovely," she said. "I'll be sure to tell your father."

"What's that?" a voice asked in the background. I grinned at the sound of my father. He was a lot less stuffy and demanding than Mom and at least followed baseball enough to get why I would be excited. I knew that if it weren't for his back being so bad, he would have made the drive himself. Instead, he has to rely on Mom to either take him somewhere or arrange for him to go.

"It's Lila," Mom said. "She won her little tournament."

"It's not a little tournament," I began.

"Said she was a *star*," Mom said, putting so much sarcastic emphasis on the word that I was fuming already.

"That's my girl," Dad said in the distance of the call.

"He's very proud of you," Mom said.

I didn't press her on her own level of pride. I already knew where it was.

"Thanks, Dad," I said.

"Mmm-hmm," Mom said, ignoring me and moving on. We had already talked about me for five seconds. It was time to get to the real reason she called. "So, anyway, the family is debating where we will go for the summer trip."

"Ahh," I said, pacing the living room. I didn't want to try to beg off the phone yet because I knew it would just mean she would call me first thing in the morning to continue, but I really just wanted to get a shower and relax. The water had just gotten to the perfect temperature. It took forever to do that.

"Uncle Marcus is dead set that we need to be near water, which I just don't understand," she said.

"Well, it is summer," I said.

"What does that have to do with it?" Mom asked. "It's always warm at beaches, who cares if it's summertime? Besides, I was told we would be doing the pyramids before I turned sixty, and I am not getting any younger."

"Mom, you're forty-eight," I said. "You have plenty of time before sixty."

"It's your father, you know," she said, ignoring me. "The man has no backbone. If Uncle Marcus suggests it, well, then that's just fine by him. I swear I never get anything I want."

"You don't, huh?" I said, but she missed every dripping drop of my sarcasm in her cross-climbing expedition.

In recent years the family had gone on a host of trips, all of which had met the approval of my mother. Expedition climbs in the Andies, Aztec ruin exploration, spending a week in Australia doing who knew what. Of course, I was not invited to those. Not if I couldn't pay my own way. Despite my mother being a somewhat wealthy person and the rest of my family being of more normal means, Mom was a big believer in everyone paying their own way. The recent summer trips had been just her and Dad until Dad's back got so bad it was harder to travel.

Then Uncle Marcus and his wife went along to Australia, more to act as caregivers than to enjoy a vacation.

Mom hated that Dad and his brother had such a close relationship, mostly because Uncle Marcus wasn't afraid to tell Mom where to stick it when she got stuck on her persecution complex.

"I have never been really, truly accepted by your father's family," she droned on. "It was always Marcus and Carl, Marcus and Carl. The boys were the important ones. I was just the add-on with money."

"Mm-hmm," I said.

"Now Marcus bought this vacation house and just *expects* that everyone will want to spend a week with him in it. As if. It's tiny, you know. Only five bedrooms. What kind of vacation house only has five bedrooms? And three bathrooms! For what I will assume will be ten people or more. You just know his wife is bringing her sister and those *nasty* children."

"Kara and Jess? Mom, they're like teenagers now."

"Yes, and rowdy and rambunctious, I am sure. Just watch for them to steal all the alcohol and play loud music and get the cops called on the house. It would be perfectly on brand for Marcus and that trashy family he married into," she said.

"Mom, they aren't trashy. They're normal people."

"Normal," Mom huffed. "That's the problem, Lila. They're normal. I married your father because he was *exceptional*. If I had known, truly known what his family was like..."

"What? You wouldn't have married him?" I laughed.

There was silence on the other end for a moment.

"At any rate," she said, brushing right past that truth bomb, "Marcus wants us all to come to the beach house, and I fear I won't be able to argue my way out of it or find some terrible disease that will give me an excuse not to go."

"Ah," I said.

"As it's a house Marcus owns, I was told that the financial requirement will be meager. Bring enough for food out and shopping. Marcus assures me he will have plenty of food in the house, but you know what that means. *Burgers. Pizza.* Nothing refined. Certainly nothing vegan."

"You're vegan now?" I asked, hope rising in my voice. I actually had gone vegan for an entire year and loved it and wanted to do it again, but bulking up for softball would have been very difficult without going back to meat.

"Heck, no," Mom said. "But you know I would rather eat alternative meat to burgers and pizza. I have to make a statement, or else no one will ever learn."

"Ahh," I said again.

"We leave on the thirtieth of June. I suspect your baseball season will be done by then?"

"Softball," I corrected, "and wait. Where is this house?"

"Myrtle Beach," she said, both with a mark of disdain and surprise. Like she had told me already.

"Mom, I just came from there," I said.

"So you said."

"Why didn't you mention that before?"

"I did, I'm sure of it. You probably weren't paying attention. Don't think I don't know when you are playing video games while on a call with me," she said.

I groaned. I had made the mistake of playing a handheld system once while Mom called when I was a teenager. I had gotten too into the game and accidentally agreed to help her unload the car from a shopping trip, then just didn't go down there when she got home. She was fuming when she found me and has not let me live it down since. I didn't even own a video game system, but it didn't stop her from assuming that every time I was talking to her on the phone, I was playing a game.

"No Mom," I said. "You never mentioned it."

"Don't call your mother a liar, dear," she said curtly. "It's classless."

"Mom," I said, summoning all my patience and strength, "I have to go."

"Oh, fine," she said. "Cut me off. Your own mother. I will speak to you again when you deem me worthy of a phone call, I suppose. Goodnight, Lila, named from my own grandmother, and who I bore for nine months in my stomach before delivering with no anesthesia."

"Good night, Mom," I said, trying to get past the long story of my birth and how revolutionary it was for her to go through and how no mother had ever suffered more. It didn't matter that I knew she'd lifted parts of the story from my cousin's birth. Or that I knew for a fact she was drugged to the moon when I was born because Dad told me.

I hung up and went back to the shower. Turning the heat back on, I went to the kitchen and pulled out the wine and a glass. I figured I was home now, and it would take a few minutes to get the water hot again. Might as well have something else to help me relax.

When the glass was empty, I disrobed and stepped in the shower again, getting as far as my entire left leg being soaked before my phone dinged again.

I groaned, reaching back to grab it but keeping my leg inside. At least this was a text. I could respond and then get in.

Oh shit.

It was Star.

Breathing out slowly, I opened the message.

"I will be home tomorrow," the message read.

I blinked.

That was it.

No indication of what time. No indication of what was going to happen when she walked in the door. No indication of how she was even getting here. I assumed she didn't need me to pick her up. But who knew?

Well, at least she'd texted me. And she wasn't coming home tonight.

I sank into the shower, tossing the phone into the sink in case someone else messaged me, the echo would be loud enough to hear in the porcelain well.

As the water began to loosen my muscles, I finally got a sense of relaxation. The aggravation of my mother faded away, as did the tightening of my muscles after an intense workout like the last couple games had been. I could feel the sand and ocean washing off my body.

But that only brought up other thoughts. Thoughts of Gavin pulling my hips down over him as my knees dug into the sand. The taste of his lips. The hardening of his cock.

How close I came to having him inside me.

How much I had wanted it.

Before I realized what I was doing, I was already touching myself. My hand slid between my thighs, and I sighed, giving in. I fantasized about that night for the first time since it happened. I let myself dream about what it could have been. Had I not stopped it.

In my dream, I slipped his cock out of his shorts and he pulled my pants off. Bare-assed, I would lower myself down on him and take him inside me. He would fill me, and I would cry out in ecstasy. He would roll me over, pressing my body into the soft sand as he claimed me for his own. Huge, heavy thrusts would bring him deeper inside me, and the sensation of the water reaching our toes while he fucked me would overwhelm my senses.

I pressed my free hand to the wall of the shower as I thought about the climax I would reach as a wave crashed behind me, barely muffling my voice.

Chapter Four

Gavin

AS EVENING STARTED to creep in, I decided to grab a shower and get into comfortable clothes. If I was going to have the place to myself, the least I could do was veg out and enjoy it. I might even skip a day of class just to let myself fully recuperate.

I turned the shower on, using my left arm because my right had gotten rather sore. The dead-armness had faded, but it was still weaker than it should be. I waited until the water got hot and slid inside, washing my hair first, then lathering up and washing my body as quickly as possible, so I had more time to just stand under the hot water.

The water pouring down on me from the shower let my mind wander. It brought up thoughts that I had tried to hide and failed spectacularly in doing. I wanted to think of anything else, but the visions of Lila were too strong. My memory was perfect. I could feel her body in my hands.

I stroked myself as my eyes closed and I gave in to the thoughts. My cock was rock hard and begging for relief. I let myself think about Lila, moving away from the memories of our beach encounter and instead, placing her in the shower with me.

In my vision, I would bring her into the water, getting her wet and dripping as I lathered up soap and caressed her. The white bubbles would slide down between her breasts, and I would pull her close. Our lips would press into each other, and slowly, I would dip down to her neck, her collarbone, her chest. I would take one wet nipple into my mouth and suck on it, making it taut as she would reach below to stroke me.

She would have to let go as I knelt down, picking up one leg and putting it over my shoulder. My lips would move down her stomach, water spraying me from above as I made my way toward her center. My tongue would slide through her folds, and she would cry out as I reached her clit. A finger would explore her, causing her to lean back against the tile and curl her body to watch me. The tip of my tongue would encourage the hood of her clit to open, and she would begin to breathe heavily as her eyes clenched shut.

I would bring her to climax, her knees buckling and legs shaking. Then I would stand. Her lips would meet mine and then begin lowering down my body. I would fill my hand with her hair as she got to her knees and ran her tongue lengthwise down my cock, swirling at the head and gathering up the pre-cum. Then she would dip it into her lips, and it would be my turn to moan heavily.

Her tongue would be warm and wet, and I would encourage her to take me deeply into her mouth. Her tongue would slide back and forth underneath as she bobbed back and forth, her big bright eyes watching my own as I reveled in the sight of my cock in her mouth. One hand would reach up to stroke me, and the other dipped between her thighs. She would moan as she touched herself, and I would feel myself getting to close to the end.

In the shower, I positioned myself with legs spread as I stroked. One arm pressed against the wall to hold myself up as my eyes clenched shut and my hand moved faster. I was so close.

Fantasy Lila stood, turning so I could bend her over and mount her. Her hands pressed against the tile to push back into me as I slid inside her. Her pussy would be wet and tight, and as I slammed into her from behind, her voice would fill the shower, and mine would rise to meet it. I would fill my hands with her ass cheeks and thrust harder and harder.

One hand would slide up to fill with her breast, and she would cry out that she wanted me to come.

My voice would change in pitch, and I would begin to roar, and she would turn around, dropping to her knees again to take me in her mouth. As I came, she would suck me, swallowing my essence and stroking me until I was empty.

In the shower, I came with the vision, crumpling down onto my own knees in the rain from above, the shower slowly getting cold as the hot water ran out. I needed to exit, but my knees were weak. It didn't help that the bruises and cuts and muscle pulls from the fight and then trying to be an elite-level pitcher forty-eight hours later were aching on every part of my body. The fantasy had been so real. The climax had been so complete. It was almost enough to make me forget all my pain.

A mixture of regret and guilt entered my mind as I shut the water off. Reaching for a towel, I tried to ward off those thoughts with various ways of explaining it to myself. She never had to know. And it was possible that she had those thoughts too. She had been dangerously close to giving in on that sand dune. It wasn't like this was one-sided.

Still, despite all of that, she was my friend. I felt guilty thinking about her that way. I dried off and then wrapped the towel around me, unworried about being seen since it would be about now that Emma was in town, meaning Kevin would be out with her.

I grabbed my phone and took it with me into the bedroom to get dressed. Shedding the towel, I reached for the drawer where I kept the sweatpants. I would have to crank up the AC a little, but for tonight, Kevin would have to deal. I didn't bother with boxers, slipping on the most comfortable pair of sweatpants I owned. Then I grabbed a long-sleeved undershirt, one usually reserved for the winter, and slipped it on too.

I liked how I looked in that shirt. It stretched to fit my muscles and made me look more impressive than I felt I was. I always wanted to wear it around Lila, just to see her reaction. That probably should have been a clue. Whenever I thought of wearing that shirt, it was always Lila's reaction first that came to mind. Then Star's.

Big, thick socks finished the ensemble, and I was already feeling a bit overheated. And hungry. I went to the window unit in my bedroom and dropped the temperature and then made my way to the living room unit to do the same. The dorm apartments were old and still had window units. I hoped I hadn't dropped them too low. If they froze, I would be getting much, much warmer over the next few weeks when Georgia went from spring to early summer.

I flopped down on the couch as gently as one can flop and opened my phone. No messages still. None from Star. None from Lila.

It was like they both just forgot I existed. Maybe they did. Maybe that was exactly what they were trying to do. After all, I was the odd man out. Their friendship pre-dated me by years. It wasn't a crazy thought that they would have both just decided to move on and swear me off for the sake of their friendship. I couldn't even be mad if they did. It would make sense.

Holding my finger over the message thread to Lila, I debated saying something to her. Something to get the conversation going again, even if it just meant she'd tell me to leave her alone. At least then I'd have answers. But I decided not to and instead swiped over to my apps.

I checked my bank account. There wasn't much left in there. Not much at all, actually.

But I was starving, I'd had a bad week, and I figured it was time to indulge myself. I had bought an entire six-pack and a case of soda before we left and stuck them in the fridge, with the thought that Kevin and I would come home champions and in the mood to celebrate with pizza and beer and soda. I would presumably have Star with me, and we would have finally consummated our relationship. I was looking forward to a Saturnalia of epic proportions.

Now I was alone.

Fuck it. I had enough in there to order pizza.

I pulled open the app for one of the three places that delivered to the dorm and started making my order. At least this way, no one would complain about the type of pizza I got. Since I was going to eat it on my own. Pineapples belonged on pizza. I was not going to have that argument with Kevin again.

Mushrooms too.

Once the pizza was ordered, I scrolled through my video streaming apps until I found the one that I had been using when I was hanging out with Lila. Despite the fact that it kind of stung to think about, I really was interested in the silly cooking show we had been watching. She had mentioned that she watched it all the time, and it was something she liked to put on to help her relax after a long day.

Figuring if it worked for her, it could work for me, I popped it on and waited for the pizza to show up. Eventually, it did, and I grabbed a few dollars cash out of the container we had by the door for delivery people and gave him his tip in that. Then I took the pizza into the living room and sat it down on the table in front of me.

What had I been thinking?

I had two pizzas, an order of cinnamon rolls, and since it was free, a two-liter of soda.

It was enough that I was pretty sure it would only be finished if I had Kevin there with me and we were mindlessly munching while watching games on TV.

Oh well. I was going to try. I wasn't going to waste any of it, that was for sure. It was probably the last time I would be able to eat out for a good long while. I was going to have to get really good at baking chicken to go in my ramen noodles.

The next episode that came on was one that Lila and I had watched when we were curled up together on her bed. Initially, I wanted to skip it. It actively hurt to think about. I didn't want to bring up any memories about her that were anything other than ones I could use for fantasy, and even then, I didn't really *want* those. They just kept popping up.

But I hit play anyway. Sitting back, I pulled back my first slice of pizza and turned off the lamp beside me. In the darkness, I ate almost the entire pizza and half of the cinnamon rolls while I watched the funny cooking show. Then, rather than going to bed, I slowly fell asleep on the couch.

I stayed that way for a couple of hours until I woke up with a terrible crick in my neck and my hip hurting. Combined with the arm and my knees, both of which had loosened up in the shower but were now back to aching, I was in pretty terrible place. Part of me regretted not going to see a doctor just so I could get some pain meds, but I knew I wouldn't take them. I refused anything the team doctor had. I wouldn't have taken them from someone in a white coat either.

Grumbling, I got up, put the food in the fridge, and shuffled my way to the medicine cabinet. Acetaminophen and water. That was going to be my medication. And then some heat gel in the morning, probably, followed by ice. Just pack my entire body in ice.

Once I had the pills down and dumped the cup in the sink, I shuffled off to bed, at least grateful that I had made it nice and cold in there, and that I wouldn't be able to smell Lila on the sheets. Not that it was going to stop me dreaming about her.

I wasn't sure anything could do that anymore.

Chapter Five

Lila

SINCE I HAD NO EARTHLY idea when Star was going to get home, I figured I might as well just go ahead and prepare for it early. Star had a tendency in recent months to vacillate between being up late and going to bed early. For as long as I had known her, she had a routine, but I had noticed since Christmas, her routine had changed and was unpredictable.

Getting up at six, I figured I would beat her no matter what. It was pretty early in the morning, and even if she managed to get home at eight or so, I would have gotten a lot done before then. Maybe she wouldn't notice, but even if she didn't, it would just mean that if we were able to work things out, it would take a while before it got crazy in there again.

First on the list was tidying up the living room and dining area. I had made sure the kitchen was spotless before I left, and though I was dying to eat something more than the peanut butter sandwich I had before bed the night before, I wanted this done first. I swept, put away the coats that I felt like were probably not going to be needed in Georgia in April, and changed the sheets that we covered the couch and loveseat with.

I put on a candle to burn in the living room and went to clean up the bathroom. It didn't take long. I had done most of all this work before I left. When I was finished, I went into the kitchen and decided to make lunch. A lunch I knew Star would like.

The thing was, I didn't know if Star was going to have eaten before she got home. If she did, there was only one thing I knew for a fact she would eat. It was the only thing she didn't eat like a bird about. Pasta.

Normally, Star had the ability to eat two pieces of celery, claim she was full, and be done with whatever dinner had for her. I hated that about her. I could eat an entire pizza and still have to hold myself back from eating ice cream too. Star could just exist off rainbows and positive thoughts sometimes.

Unless there was pasta.

It was one of the very few vices that girl had. It wasn't like she was Italian either. She just loved noodles, especially spaghetti when I made a sauce from somewhat scratch. We had a box of frozen hamburgers in the freezer, and I grabbed a couple of those to warm up while I collected spices and got the water boiling. Then I cooked the meat in the pan with onions, green peppers, and carrots, added garlic, and put a couple cans of diced tomatoes in.

Then I left it alone.

It would cook as long as it took for Star to get home. The longer the better. Of course, the noodles would be done and probably in the fridge if she took more than an hour.

As the food cooked, my stomach again reminded me I hadn't eaten, and I decided I could probably sneak a plate of it for myself and she wouldn't notice. I was lucky that my only class of the day was virtual. I could literally open my laptop and knock out the class at any time. So I piled a plate with pasta and sauce, sat down at the table, and opened up the laptop, doing two things at once and feeling pretty accomplished about my day so far.

Once the class was done, I cleaned up the kitchen from the mess of making the sauce and then... sat.

I didn't know what else to do. Star didn't mention when she was getting home, and it was ten now. She could be hours away. She could be right outside of the door. There was no way of knowing. I didn't want to get comfortable and watch TV or go for a walk or anything. I wanted to be waiting for her. I wanted to get this conversation, whatever it was going to be, out of the way immediately.

I tried to envision how it would go. I hoped she would walk in, like she had other times when she was in a bad mood, and be distracted by the pasta sauce smell. It was a trick I had devised before by trial and error. She would have texted or called, and I could tell she was in a bad place. So I cooked spaghetti. When she came home, it seemed to instantly improve her mood.

But would it work over *this*? I mean, she could see this as me trying to steal her boyfriend from her. I didn't know if pasta had the required power to smooth over someone stealing your lover.

I shuddered.

I didn't like thinking of the connotations of them being 'lovers.' Not that I had any claim to him. Ugh. It was all so complicated.

I paced for a while, going over different approaches to the conversation. I could try to talk first, intercepting her if she came in hot. I knew she couldn't do anything physical and probably wouldn't try. She was bound to know she could be snapped in half by a strong wind, much less someone with my athletic strength. I could hold my own against biker guys, slinging giant rocks at them. A five-foot-one girl who struggled to lift five-foot canvases was not likely to be a physically imposing match, even if I tied a hand behind my back.

Still, I wouldn't want to hurt her either. Especially since I kind of felt like I was the bad guy here.

I would try to start out with an apology. Yes, that seemed right. I would start speaking by saying that first off, I was sorry. And that before anything was said, I wanted to make sure we stayed friends, if that was possible. That no man could get between our friendship.

Of course, the fact that I couldn't stop thinking about Gavin might make that a small lie, but I wasn't going to address that yet.

If she came in sad, that was my nightmare. How was I going to handle a crying, hurt Star? It would be like I had kicked a puppy. I had seen her sad once before, and she was like a lost deer. You couldn't help but want to help her. With her big eyes and long lashes and golden hair, she looked like a doll. You just wanted to pick her up, tuck her in bed, and bring her tea and cookies.

But if she was sad because of something *I* did, ugh. What to do then? *How do I make her feel better when I'm the reason she felt bad?*

I was still going over the options, settling on one or two approaches depending on how she seemed when she came in, when I heard the key rattle in the door.

I froze.

And promptly forgot everything I had decided in the meantime.

Shit, shit, shit, what was I going to say?

Shit.

The door opened, and the first thing I saw were two suitcases, wheeled in. Then several bags hanging off an arm that was elbowing the door open. The suitcases and bags, predictably, were dropped just inside the door, and the door shut as Star pulled her key and locked it from the inside. Then she turned.

And ran to me with a giant smile on her face and leapt through the air, completely disregarding her own safety, in a bearhug.

"Oh, Lila, I missed you! It's so good to see you!"

She kissed me on my cheek and held me tightly, like a baby koala, until I hugged her back. It was times like this that I felt even less feminine. Here was Star, a full-grown woman, wrapped around me like a child to their mother.

"Hey," I finally choked out.

"Oh, gosh, Lila! My trip was *so* amazing. I have to tell you all about it, but first, hold on. I have to show you... wait. Is that spaghetti?"

"Y-yes," I said, stunned and unsure of myself. This was not how I planned any of this.

"You are. The. Best. Oh my goodness. I can't wait. I am *starving*. I didn't eat on the plane because everything they had was so salty, but I will absolutely demolish a plate of your pasta sauce. Speaking of! I had a really interesting pasta on my layover in Italy. Did you know they have like a zillion different kinds of pasta? Some of them have the same names as here, but they look so different. It's crazy! Oh, shit, I should have brought some home. I could have bought a bunch, but then I would have to carry it through customs. I bet a lot of people do that, though. Don't you think? It's probably a big thing to buy pasta in Italy and bring it home."

She was rambling, and I was at least three sentences behind her, trying desperately to catch up in my confusion. Sweeping in her graceful, ballet-like way, she went into the kitchen and removed a plate. She was the only person I knew who could get those ceramic plates out of a cabinet without making any noise. It was like her hands sucked up the sound.

Placing the plate on the counter, she grabbed a massive mound of pasta with the tongs and placed it on the plate, her lips still moving and more of the story of her trip flowing out. Covering the pasta with sauce and then cheese, she took it with her to the living room, plopping down on the loveseat and continuing to talk as she twirled some pasta on a fork.

"...and then, Lila, you will love this, the guy that we were using as an interpreter said, 'but I'm a Gemini!'"

I laughed nervously, knowing I'd missed the part of the story that would have made that make sense, but Star didn't seem to notice. She was busy laughing at the story herself. When she finished laughing, she seemed to notice the room for the first time and turned to look at me.

"You did some cleaning, didn't you?"

"I did," I mumbled.

"Looks nice. Smells nice too. That reminds me! We went to this amazing candle store just outside of Paris. It had candles that looked like penises! It was so funny. I took some pictures to send you, but I forgot. You know me. I get distracted easily, right?"

She had no idea just how easily, apparently.

"Heh, heh," I mustered.

"I was tempted to buy one, but then I'd have to explain a penis in my luggage to Customs, and that would be *way* harder than explaining pasta, I think. Anyway, after the candle shop, we went to this club. It stayed open all night, and we danced the entire time. It was amazing, Lila. I had no idea what time it was when I was leaving, but when we went outside it was the middle of the afternoon! We had danced for like fifteen hours! I was so tired. But then Miranda suggested we go get some wine and head home, and we stopped at this lovely little café."

She continued her story for a few more minutes, with me barely able to keep up and pay any attention at all. At no point during any of this had she mentioned the text messages. Or breaking up with Gavin. Or the whole long message I'd sent that she simply responded 'ok' to. Did she just not remember? Was her brain so flighty that she literally didn't remember?

"So," she said, finally stopping for a breath. "What did you do for your vacation?"

My jaw dropped.

Chapter Six

Gavin

I NEVER MADE IT TO the bed.

As I shuffled down the hall, my knee, which had been hurting since the fight in the parking lot, gave out. It was just a minor thing, but it hurt like a son of a bitch, and I went down pretty hard. I knew that in situations like this, I didn't know how bad the injury was, and if I tried to push it, I could hurt it a lot worse.

So, scooting on my backside, I made it to the couch again and pulled down the blanket we always kept on the back. Kevin was a big couch-napper, and because of it, he always had a pillow and a blanket nearby. Considering he was as tall as a damn tree, it was pretty comical to come in and see his giant frame curled up as best he could. Now I was just thankful for the routine, since it allowed me to get some sleep in a little more comfort.

I turned the TV back on and set it to the classic sports channel. It was playing a game from the early eighties, and the lack of loud music, chyron graphics, and sort of monotonous, radio-friendly play-by-play helped lull me to sleep pretty easily. The game had just started when I dozed off, and when I snapped awake to the sound of Kevin coming home, it was in the bottom of the eighth.

"Hey, bud, sorry I woke you up," Kevin said from the kitchen where he was filling a glass with water.

"It's cool," I said. "My knee went out, so I couldn't make it to the bed, and I just figured I'd catch some shut-eye here. What time is it?"

"Three," Kevin said, barely containing a giggle.

"Three? In the morning?"

"Yeah, sorry again, boss," he said, looking wildly un-sorry. "I didn't mean to come in so late. Definitely didn't mean to wake you up."

"It's good, bro," I said. "You have a good time with Emma?"

"Oh man," he said, grinning like a child who has just been handed a credit card in a video game store, "the best. The absolute best."

"Good to hear," I said, sitting up and rubbing my knee. It felt a lot better. I probably could try to get back to my bedroom on it now, and part of me desperately wanted to get back to sleep, but Kevin seemed awake and like he wanted to talk. I'd be a bad friend if I bailed on him.

"She's so great," Kevin said. "Like the best."

"So this thing might have legs then?" I asked.

"I think... I think so," Kevin said. "I mean, it's early, but if it were up to me, then yeah, for sure. She's really sweet and lively as all hell. We have very similar tastes."

"I gathered that," I said. "Seems like you two were two peas in a pod at the beach."

"We were," he said. "I was trying not to completely bail on you after the fight, but she was... insatiable. And frankly, so was I. And you seemed like you were in good hands with Lila and all. Speaking of..."

Here we go. We hadn't talked about this situation yet, though I knew he knew something was up. I guess I really didn't have much of a choice now.

"Yeah, about that," I said, sighing. "That might take a little time to explain."

"Well," Kevin said, "I don't have early morning class. I know you don't. If you're down, I'm down. I don't think I'm getting to sleep anytime soon."

"Fair enough," I said, shaking the last of the cobwebs out of my mind. "I might need a beer, though."

"On it," Kevin said, standing and going to the kitchen. "Hey. Wait a minute. Did you have Lila over tonight? Oh shit, is she here?"

"No," I said quickly, "no, nothing like that. Much sadder than that."

"Oh, boss, don't tell me you ate all this shit yourself?"

I nodded.

"Dude. All right, I'm bringing beer. You want a slice? Looks like you got some left."

"No," I said. "I'm good. You're free to some if you want."

"Pineapple?"

"I ate the one with pineapple," I said. "The deal was for one two-topping and one one-topping. I got pepperoni for the other."

"Fantastic," he said. "Give me just a sec."

I watched as Kevin piled a midnight snack, er, well, a three in the morning snack, onto his plate. It was roughly half the pizza. Then he stuck it in the microwave, nuked it for twenty seconds, and came back with the remaining four beers out of the six-pack.

"Here you go," he said, cracking open one of the bottles with his bare hands. I never saw him use a bottle opener. When you catch hundred-mile-an-hour fastballs all the time, I suppose a beer bottle lid doesn't hold much challenge.

"Thanks," I said. "Before I begin with anything, I just wanted to say, I am terribly happy for you and Emma. I hope that you guys have a ton of fun and wish you nothing but the best."

"I'll drink to that," he said.

"I think you'd drink to anything at this point," I laughed.

"All right, so, let's start at the beginning. When we left for the trip, you said Star was supposed to come and then wasn't. So fill me in from there."

"Didn't we talk about this already?" I asked.

He shrugged.

"I might not have paid very much attention if we did. Recap it."

I sighed.

"Star decided at the last minute, and I do mean the last minute, that she wasn't coming. That's why I was so hyped and then so bummed when we left. I was looking forward to us kind of becoming a real couple over the week, you know?"

"So it wasn't... real yet?" he asked, cocking his eyebrow.

"No, weirdly," I said. "She's a weird duck, man. Super flirty, all that, but then just kind of shies away when things get even remotely close to intense. I don't know what was up with that, but I was really looking forward to being alone with her, not just for *that*, but to really get to know her. I always felt like there was some distance there."

"I get that," he said. "You always talked about her in a really superficial way. How pretty she was, how talented she was, etc. Never something she actually *said*. Or *did*."

I nodded.

"That would have been good insight to know a week ago," I laughed.

"So what happened this week?" Kevin said, sitting back into the loveseat and taking a sip of his drink while putting one arm back behind his head.

"Well, she didn't really message me when she left or when she landed. I was kind of in the dark about what she was up to. It wasn't like we had done anything or established many boundaries or anything, but it felt like... I don't know. It felt like she was being sneaky or something. Like she wanted to be free while she was in France and do whatever she wanted, with *whoever* she wanted."

"Ahh," he said. "Artists."

I shrugged.

"At any rate, Lila got sick, and I went and brought her soup and some cards and dice and stuff. I ended up hanging out there all evening and then fell asleep on the bed beside her watching this show on her phone."

"Clothed?" Kevin asked, his eyebrow peaked.

"Yes," I said firmly. "She was sick. I was helping her out because she's my friend. Nothing more."

"Except..."

I sighed.

"Man, I don't know. It was nice. I mean, yeah, she felt like shit, but it was still just *nice* to hang out with her, you know?" He nodded sagely. "I like her company. I think she's funny. Even sick she's kind of adorable."

"Let me ask you something before you continue," he said.

"Sure."

"If Star said she was sick, and she was going to stay in, would your first instinct be to bring her soup and hang out with her?"

"Well, no, I'd give her space..."

"Uh huh," he said, nodding. "Continue."

I took a swig of my drink, peeling the label off as I went.

"Well, she got better, and when she went out with us, we got to dancing."

"I saw that," Kevin said. "I mean, I wasn't paying attention, since I was there with Emma, but I happened to see you two grinding."

"It didn't last long," I said. "But it was hot. I'm not going to lie. And there was a moment there that it felt like... man, it felt like we were going to start making out. And then I got barreled into, and the fight started in the bar."

"And you two ran off, which you should have by the way, I'm not knocking it. You needed to get out of there."

"Yeah," I said. "We ran off, and when the fight in the parking lot happened, she jumped right in."

Kevin laughed.

"Boss, she was *slinging* those rocks. They were like bullets whipping past." He made a whistling sound, followed by slapping his hands together to mimic the sound. I smirked and nodded.

"She was laying them in, for sure," I said. "Then we got back to my room, and after you guys left, she hung out, and we fell asleep together again." His eyebrow peaked again, and I shook my head. "Still clothed. Well, sort of. I didn't have my shirt and was in my shorts, but you know. Anyway, I got up in the middle of the night because it was starting to get to me, you know?"

"What was? The fight? Or Lila?"

"Both. Everything. My parents being losers and getting me into that trouble, Star being gone and not seeming to care when I called her and told her what happened. Like, she acted like I was bothering her, and she was clearly in some club. It was like four in the morning over there."

"You called her?"

"Yup," I said. "She knew Lila was there too. But she didn't seem upset about that, or about me getting my ass kicked. She was upset she got pulled away from whatever she was doing. And I could clearly hear the thumping in the background of loud music."

"Weird," Kevin said. "I mean, it's Star, so maybe not weird, but weird for normal people."

"Anyway, I went out to the beach in the middle of the night to think about shit, and Lila must have woken up and come down there to find me. But when we did, I told her I was breaking up with Star and then we made out."

"Spicy," Kevin said, leaning forward in his chair. "How far did it go?"

I loved that he had no problems asking me that. Most people would know a boundary would be there, but Kevin was my best friend. Boundaries were for other people.

"Almost too far," I said. "No clothes came off, but it was damn close, and then she just hopped up and ran back to her room."

"Ah," he said. "Got cold feet. Guilty feet, maybe."

"Something like that," I said. "But then she didn't talk to me the rest of the trip. Not one word."

"Did you try to talk to her?"

"Well, no," I said. "But she's the one who ran away."

Kevin sighed. "I know, it's not the old days and I'm not supposed to say you're supposed to chase her and all, but, in this case, I think you were supposed to chase her."

"Really?"

"I mean, I think?" Kevin said. "But before you do that, you absolutely *need* to talk to Star. You know that, right? You need to be real clear with her about where you two stand."

"Yeah," I said. "I know."

"Just make sure there's no hard feelings if you asked Lila out. If she was upset about you calling her and filling her in on life, maybe she didn't think of your relationship as seriously as you did. She might be cool with it. But you need to make sure of that before you talk to Lila again."

"You're right," I said.

"Whatever you do, just make sure Star doesn't take out any frustration on Lila. Be the bigger person. Take that hit for her. If you really like her, make sure you take that hit for her."

I nodded. I was already thinking the same thing, but it was nice to hear it from someone else, especially someone I trusted as much as I trusted Kevin.

"All right, boss," he said, downing the last of his drink. "I'm going to put another one of these away, but you should get to bed and get some sleep. You look like shit."

I laughed.

"Is it the eye?"

He nodded.

"And everything else. Go to fucking bed, boss."

"On my way," I said, standing. "Goodnight, brother."

"Goodnight, boss," he said.

Feeling a little bit lighter, I headed to bed, making a mental note to contact both of the girls tomorrow. I needed to set things straight and be honest about how I felt. Especially about Lila.

Chapter Seven

Lila

I LAID IN BED AND STARED at my ceiling for a long time going over everything.

None of it made much sense.

Either Star was the most artsy-space-brained person in the history of mankind or the worst person on the planet. Or maybe just the best friend on the planet. I wasn't entirely sure, and the more I thought about it, the more confused I got, and the worse I felt about the whole situation. And the more creeped out I got about it.

The words she chose were... interesting.

We sat down to eat the spaghetti lunch, and I listened to her continue to tell me how amazing the countryside of France was for a good little bit of time. Then she talked about projects she got ideas for while she was out there, described a few paintings she made that she was having shipped back home and wouldn't be there for a few more days, and then slipped into a happy, contented silence as she slurped her noodles.

Finally, I worked up the courage to ask about the texts.

"Oh, I never thought we were serious anyway," she had said, between poking at the pasta and then swirling it around her fork and stuffing it into her mouth. "I was busy having fun in France. It barely registered, honestly."

"It barely registered?" I asked, feeling like my entire life was a lie at that point. Why had I put myself through so much torture if she didn't *care*?

Because you are a good person, my brain frantically tried to tell itself. *You did the right thing because you didn't know.*

"I mean, yeah," she said. "Like I said. I was busy. Paris was fun, girl."

She had stopped short of saying she did anything with anyone over there. No blatant admissions of cheating, or even anything that could be halfway looked at as cheating considering the apparent gray area her relationship with Gavin was in. But even if she did, she wouldn't have seen it as cheating because they weren't exclusive. I wasn't even entirely sure Star saw herself as the kind of person capable of, and thus being expected to be, exclusive to anyone.

She was Star. The artist. The free spirit.

When I mentioned the text, I was expecting the mood shift, or at least some acknowledgement that would bring us into a more serious tone. Instead, she had laughed. Her light, flighty little laugh that she did when I mentioned things like bills that needed to be paid. As if the worldly worries of mere mortals are far below the lofty thoughts of a true artist.

"No boy could get between us, Lila," she had said later. "You should know that. I'm glad you *had fun*."

She had put the same emphasis on the same words she had used about her trip to Paris. *Had fun.* Whatever that was supposed to mean.

Maybe it was supposed to be vague. She didn't want to get into the particulars of what she might or might not have done and with whom on her trip, nor did she want to get into the particulars of what Gavin and I might have done in Myrtle Beach. She was apparently willing to see both escapades as similar and not worthy of getting into detail about.

I wasn't sure how I felt about any of that.

Now I was questioning everything. Was she just saying all that to take care of her own ego? I mean, Star was objectively gorgeous. And talented. She had that appeal that people couldn't not pay attention to. A certain draw to her. She was, as her name implied, a star.

So having Gavin suddenly wanting to be with me had to be a bit of a kick to the ego, didn't it? Even if I was the large athlete who towered over her and didn't have the spritely figure she had, a guy that was interested in her had become interested in me. That must have gotten to her, didn't it?

Or did she just think that Gavin was only interested in me in the absence of her? Like she thought that if she wanted him back at any point, all she had to do was show interest and clearly, I would be left in the dust? Maybe that was part of it. Maybe she pitied me that I thought I had something with someone who she barely even registered as being part of her life?

Or none of it was true, and she was genuinely that space-brained that she didn't even put together that Gavin would expect that they had some kind of relationship going on that would be damaged by her skipping off to France and not particularly being interested in him spending as much time with me as he was.

I tried to close my eyes and go to sleep, but the day just kept rolling over and over in my head. I couldn't seem to come to any conclusions, and it bugged me. I just wanted some form of straight answer from Star, and while she seemed to give me one, it still felt... wrong somehow. Like it was fake. She was putting on a show for some reason. Why, I didn't know.

Turning onto my side, I pulled open my phone and mindlessly scrolled over to my messages. My thumb hovered over the conversation with Gavin. I wanted to text him. I wanted to start some kind of dialogue with him, maybe discuss Star and how weird she had been acting. It was crazy how often we had talked in the last few weeks. How much I relied on those texts from him to brighten bad days or give me motivation to get things done so I could keep up the correspondence. How excited I had been just to hang out with him when we were having the tournament, even with Star there.

Then, nothing.

It was like something critical was missing from my life now, which was ridiculous. We had only started texting occasionally right after he started tutoring me. It picked up as I tried to give him pointers on Star and then went insane when they started dating and we became friends. But the more I thought about it, the more I wondered if it had ever really been a friendship between us or if it had always been a prelude to this.

Angrily, I swiped away from the messages. How could I be so dumb? How could I have gotten myself into this stupid mess?

I settled on a game for a few minutes, crushing candy absentmindedly and hoping it would tire me out or at least get me to not think for a few minutes. It did neither. Hitting the home button, I scrolled to the streaming service I used most and pulled it up.

And there was the show Gavin and I had been watching when I was sick in bed, and then again when he was beaten up and needed to rest. It had been one of my favorite shows. Now I didn't think I could watch it without emotion creeping up at the corners of my eyes.

I hit play anyway.

For a few minutes, I felt my breath catch as I watched an episode I remembered us watching together. I hit skip to the next one and then again until I got to one I was sure we hadn't watched, or at least might have been playing while we were sound asleep. I lay in bed and watched it for almost the entire episode before finally feeling like my eyes were drifting shut, and I paused it, letting the phone fall onto my mattress as I fell asleep.

I dreamed that Star and I were making a cake ourselves, but a challenge was defying us. We had to make it in the shape of Gavin's face.

And no matter how many times we got it almost right, I would ruin it. Star would just keep asking me why I had to screw it up.

And I had no answer for her.

When the alarm went off in the morning, thankfully a regularly set one since I hadn't bothered to check and make sure I had one set to wake me up, I groggily turned it off and sat up on my knees from my stomach and tried to will myself to consciousness.

Restful sleep had eluded me, my dreams were stress nightmares, I had gotten overheated and was sick to my stomach, and I was low-key terrified I was going to just run into Gavin in the street on my way to class. Not to mention not knowing if Star was really okay, or if she was going to be standing in the living room with a beautifully created effigy of me and a couple hundred sharp implements.

I tried to shake it all off and went to the bathroom to brush my teeth and get ready. When I came out a few minutes later, I felt some semblance of being a normal human being and got dressed for a day of classes.

Georgia in spring was a confusing mess. Some days it was still breezy and sunny, and a hoodie would be fine if it was light, as long as you wore something decent underneath. Some days it was blazingly hot, which meant the rooms in the schools would have the air cranked to deep frost, meaning you needed to pack a parka just to survive in class but wear spaghetti straps to not die in the heat. Other days, it was oppressively humid outside, and there was a constant chance for rain to break it up with a torrential downpour, but otherwise, you wanted to wear as little clothing as was legally possible to stave off the moisture buildup.

I checked the weather app. Eighty-six with ninety-four percent humidity. Fifty percent chance of rain.

Great.

I had a pair of short-shorts that I rarely ever wore in the daylight hours because I was fairly certain the bottom of my ass cheeks showed.

It was a rather common style, especially in a college town, but I wasn't usually brave enough to rock it. Still, it meant less ass-sweat, so I threw them on. One of the college T-shirts, showing our mascot, was light enough to not make me hotter. My umbrella would be by the door. I'd have to pray I got to class without soaking the shirt through.

Closing the door as lightly as I could so I didn't wake up the usually late-sleeping Star, I turned when I heard it click and got two steps before I stopped dead in my tracks.

Star was sitting in the living room, looking at her phone. She looked like she was staring at something rather intently, and her brows were furrowed. She often looked like that when she was painting or making something out of clay or something, but just looking down at a phone like that was weird. Then she looked up.

Her expression when she saw me was hard to read. It was certainly an expression, not a passive face, but I couldn't quite tell if it was shock, anger, or joy. Or some weird mix of the three. Then she broke out into what I could only describe as a politician's smile. It was wide and showed all her teeth and was most certainly unnatural.

Fake. It was a fake smile.

"Gooooood morning!" she said in a sing-song voice.

"Uhh, good morning?" I said.

She hopped up to her feet, pranced over to me, looked back over her shoulder for a moment like she was making sure she hadn't forgotten anything, then looked back at me.

Suddenly she reached out one finger, tapped me on the nose and said, "Boop."

With that, she slipped into her room, shut the door, and locked it.

I stood there, staring at her door for a moment in complete confusion.

What the hell was that?

I must have stood there for a full minute before I shook myself out of the fog it had put me in, calmed my heart from beating into my throat, and made a shuffling quick-step into the kitchen to grab a water and a protein bar. I wasn't going to stand there and make breakfast of any type, not just because I didn't have the time, but also because I frankly wanted to get the hell out of there.

As I shut the door behind me, I could just hear her bedroom door open again. She had hidden from me. Run away from me. For... reasons.

What in the blue hell was going on?

Hesitantly, I took a few steps away and tried to just go to class and forget about it. I'd figure out more when I got home.

Chapter Eight

Gavin

I WAS PRETTY SURE I might fail any quiz that I would be given this week in this class.

The professor was an older man with one of those monotone voices that made me think of the adults in the *Peanut's* cartoons. Technically, he was saying words, but they all sounded like the same three syllables said at the same tempo with the same length of note. After a few seconds, my eyes just wanted to shut, and my brain wanted to turn off for a while. He was a human quaalude.

Besides, I was too distracted by my phone.

Usually, being distracted by my phone wasn't a problem for me. I simply didn't ever take it out of my pocket unless I was making notes in it or using the calculator. I was pretty good at not dicking around on it in classes, one of the reasons I had great grades. But sometimes with Professor Snoreface, I would bring it out and have something interesting to do so I could pick it up and remind my brain that it needed to be awake. It didn't always work, but it worked enough.

This time though, my phone wasn't being used as a wake-up device. I was actively paying attention to it. Because I had finally taken the first step. I had texted Star.

It had been first thing this morning, and I was fairly sure that meant she wouldn't be getting back to me for a while. She wasn't the world's earliest riser, nor was she the type of person to text back immediately when she saw you had texted her. Any number of things could get in the way and make her lose her attention to it. Including a particularly pretty raindrop.

Seriously, that had been an excuse before, and Lila had backed her up. She even took a picture of Star standing by the window, staring intently at the drop of water as it fell down their window.

In the text, I had been as clear as I could be, and as apologetic as I could be too. I had told her rather clearly, my side of the story, starting from the disappointment I felt that she clearly didn't seem to think our relationship was as close as I had thought it was when she bailed on the trip. It had been difficult to write that part, because I didn't want to feel accusatory. It had been my miscalculation that we were closer than I thought we were. She didn't have blame there.

But then I got into how close Lila and I had gotten as friends, and that when she was sick, I was compelled to take care of her. That we grew closer. That I had been struggling with the feelings of how close I felt to her for a long time.

Then I told her that we had kissed on the beach after my text to her. That Lila had run away not long after, feeling guilty and hadn't spoken to me since. That she was clearly choosing her friendship with Star over whatever was possible between the two of us, and that I understood it. I begged her not to take it out on Lila. That I had fallen for her roommate, but that she shouldn't hold it against her.

Then I said that if they both just wanted to close this chapter of their lives, to forget about me, I understood. But that I was going to try and contact Lila. Because the feelings I had for her were so very much deeper than just one kiss on a beach.

It had been a pouring-heart situation, and I felt better when it was sent. At least now the whole story was out. There was nothing left unsaid, no secrets, nothing that I could feel like I still needed to say. She was going to respond to it however she felt like. Which included not responding, I guessed. But it kept me on pins and needles, and as the class droned on around me, I waited and waited for the three little dots indicating she was typing. I wanted to give her time to message me before I messaged Lila.

Eventually, I found myself dozing off, eyes closing as they looked at the phone and only waking up when the sounds of the other students filing out of the lecture hall snapped me awake in mild panic. I had no clue what the lecture had been on. No clue what the professor said outside of "please be seated." And Kevin wasn't there. Usually, he was sitting in class nearby if not right beside me, and I had to elbow him awake a few times over the course of the hour.

But with Kevin nowhere to be seen, and I would bet that nowhere was Emma's bedroom, I was alone and noteless. I was sure I could turn on the 'star baseball player charm' and ask one of the more studious girls in the class for a copy of their notes, but I felt guilty about doing that. It would be better to just be honest with the professor and tell him I dozed off in his class and needed notes. He might give me crap for it, but I was sure he'd help me out. I aced his class all the time anyway.

The next class I had was an hour later, so I took a break to shake the cobwebs out and get a protein shake. After the next class would be my normal workout time, and while most of my body was still sore as hell, and I was under strict no-throwing rules from Coach for the next week, I could at least get some cardio in. But I would need something on my stomach other than the pizza and beer from the night before.

I stopped at the cafeteria and went to the little shake place they had opened up last semester. They were ridiculously expensive, but they were terrific shakes, and adding protein to them only cost an extra fifty cents or so. As I paid for it, I tried doing a little mental math about what I had left and how long it was going to last me. I had already texted Coach about finding a job that would allow me the flexibility to play and do my classes, something he had told us all to do if we found ourselves needing more income. I hoped he would text me back soon. I wasn't going to make it long without it.

My next class was a breeze, busywork mostly. Math always made sense to me, mostly because as a kid, I simply figured out how to translate it into baseball problems. The numbers didn't change meanings. Words, now they could be tricky, but numbers were consistent. A six was a six. None of that their, they're, there stuff.

I was coming out of that class, heading to the gym before my last class of the day when I checked the phone again. Still nothing from Star. Nothing from Coach, for that matter. It made my nerves twang. I felt like I was on the edge of a cliff, waiting to find out how hard the breeze was going to be. I needed someone to talk to about it, and I didn't want to bother Kevin. He was in the throes of a new relationship, and I didn't want to bring him down talking about all my stress.

Besides, I knew what he would say. *Be patient. Wait for Star to talk. Then talk to Lila.*

Ugh.

I hated waiting.

The gym was packed to the gills. Apparently enough people had partied over spring break and now needed to work off the excess calories that there wasn't a free elliptical machine or standard treadmill in sight. No jump ropes available, nothing. Just free weights that I couldn't use, and even those were being taken up by muscle bros who thought that biceps were the end-all be-all of physical fitness.

I waited my turn to hit one of the treadmills and then stuck my earbuds in. Twenty minutes of running and I was bored, still didn't see a chance to do anything more intense of a workout for a while, and was so damn on edge I felt like I might snap in half. I needed to do something. And running wasn't it.

If I could have punched a punching bag, that would have been great. But Coach had eyes everywhere, and if I violated the *no fucking around with your shoulder* rule, I was going to hear about it until the end of time. So I packed my things up, having barely broken a sweat, and headed for the door more frustrated than I had been when I came in.

I needed to make a move. There was no two ways about it. Kevin would kill me, but I had to go against my friend's advice. I needed to go straight to the source. I needed to contact Lila.

I pulled open her messages as I wandered in the direction of my last class. It still wasn't for another half hour, but it was central to everything in what passed for downtown and was only a short walk from my apartment. I could hang out nearby until class just to be close, and the student commons weren't far away if I got overheated in the excessively humid atmosphere.

When I reached the benches in the shade by the commons, I pulled the messages up again and sighed. Here goes nothing.

"Can we meet somewhere and talk?" I texted.

I headed into the commons, deciding I'd rather have the air conditioning and cluster of people than the relative quiet of outside but feeling like I would sweat through my clothes. As soon as I got inside, the air blasted me, and I felt a little bit better. I was at least being proactive.

My phone dinged.

Well, that was fast.

I pulled it up to eye level and read the return message.

"Yes. Tonight, if possible."

I couldn't help but feel a thrill run up my back. Maybe it was just cold air hitting the sweat running down my spine, but it felt a lot more visceral than that. My stomach clenched, too, and I was positive it had nothing to do with the shake. This was all Lila and my desire to see her again. In person.

"My place?" I asked. "Kevin will be at Emma's all night."

"I know," she typed back.

I laughed.

I was sure Emma had blown up her phone to talk about the budding relationship with Kevin. Emma was a sweet girl but one of those people that didn't have a personal information bubble. She would tell anyone about her personal life, and I gathered that her close friends got the really juicy details, whether they wanted them or not.

"Seven?" I typed back.

"Sure," she responded.

I looked at the time on my smartwatch. It was four. Class was an hour and a half and started in a half an hour. That wouldn't give me a lot of time to get home, change, and get the place ready for company.

I was going to have to skip class.

Oh, well. It was worth it.

Grinning from ear to ear, I stuffed the phone into my pocket and headed back toward the apartment. Tonight had to go perfectly. That meant the place had to be as spotless as I could make it, and either I needed to make dinner or have something delivered. Kevin was just going to have to deal with me being a few bucks short on rent next month.

Either that, or Coach was going to have to find a job for me in the next week that I could get paid under the table at. Because I wasn't going to cheap out tonight. Not if this was my one shot.

Chapter Nine

Lila

IT WAS MISERABLE OUTSIDE. Horribly miserable.

I just wanted to go home, strip off these clothes that were now hermetically sealed to my body, take the coldest shower ever, put on soft cotton, and sit directly in front of the air conditioner until it was time to leave for Gavin's. I would have, too, if it weren't for the fact that I was frankly completely confused about Star.

Also kind of frightened.

The problem was, she had been acting weird all day. The thing in the morning was strange enough, but when I stopped back by the apartment to drop off the books I didn't need and pick up my laptop charger, she ran away again to her room. This time, I saw her with what looked like a few paint brushes, so at least it was a little less terrifying, but who knew what she was painting?

What was I going to say to her?

"Hi, roomie, I'm heading over to your recent ex-boyfriend's place, who you split up with after he kissed me on a beach and also, we rubbed our bodies on each other a bunch. But we are totally just going to *talk*. I put some bagel pizzas in the freezer!"

It just didn't have the right ring to it.

Besides, the last time I went to go *talk* to Gavin, we'd ended up doing the aforementioned body rubbing and kissing. There was simply no good way of telling her about it, no good way of phrasing it, quite possibly pushing her completely over the edge into whatever it was she was doing.

Still, I really wanted to change clothes.

When I got to the apartment, the living room was quiet. I opened the door slowly, trying not to make much noise as I made my way to my room. As I passed her door, I could hear her inside, listening to music softly and moving around in there. I smiled.

At least that was normal. Star often put on music and went to dance in her room. She would sometimes open the door, sweaty and partially clothed, the smell of scented candles wafting out, a big smile on her face and talking about chakras or some such. Whenever she did that, she was usually pretty easy to get along with for a few days, more centered and grounded. Then she would slowly lose touch with reality again and start only talking about art.

If she was in there dancing to music, I could safely assume that things were probably okay. She was either channeling her energy into an artistic piece or simply blowing off steam. It made me feel a lot better.

I went into my room, stripped down, and jumped in the shower, enjoying having lukewarm water to cool me off. The stress of the day had been building, and as thankful as I was to get into water that was cooler than I had felt all day, I slowly found myself inching the heat up bit by bit and sinking into the muscle-relaxing nature of it pounding on my shoulders. If there was a top favorite thing about this apartment, it was the water pressure. It was like tiny little hammers, flying out of the showerhead and beating on my muscles until they relaxed.

When I got out, I slipped into the bedroom, wearing just my towel, and opened the closet door. I had a few dresses in there, but most of them were rather formal and not exactly the kind of message I wanted to send. Which got me wondering, what kind of message exactly was it I was trying to get across?

I could go for professional, maybe some slacks and a nice shirt. Distant but cordial. Or I could go for a sundress, something light and airy, giving off the impression that I wasn't worried, just looking to clear the air. Or I could put on my combat boots, the one little black dress I owned, do the heavy eyeshadow, and go for a neutral chaos look, one that was prepared for every eventuality.

Settling on the sundress and sneakers, I spent more time than I would have admitted to anyone else on whether I wanted to wear bicycle shorts or panties underneath. And if I was going to wear panties, if they were going to be white and normal or some other color and distinctly sexier. Not that the sexiness would be for Gavin's benefit. I had no intention of him seeing anything underneath my dress at all. But maybe it would give me a bit more confidence going in.

Let's face it. Gavin was fucking *hot.* And I was... well, I was me.

Nothing like Star.

Speaking of, I noticed that the music was gone, replaced by the unnerving silence again. I thought about the morning when I had come out of the room and she was creepily sitting in the living room in the silence and shuddered. Hopefully she wasn't pulling that again. Or worse, trying to cook.

The stories of Star's attempts at culinary expertise were varied, horrifying, and repetitive. She could burn water. She was the only person I knew who was completely baffled by cooking rice. It ended up being blackened chunks that took forever to get off the bottom of the pot. And she used way too much garlic powder in *everything*. One thing was for sure: For all Star's weirdnesses, she most certainly was not a vampire.

Opting for the sexy black panties that I wore on test days to do the same trick of making myself confident, I got dressed and did my makeup as delicately as I could. I had watched Star put on her makeup, sitting on the couch, only occasionally looking at her reflection in her phone. I was not so brave. I had a mirror, a backup mirror, a concave mirror, and a bunch of makeup remover for the moments where I absolutely massacred my own face. It was an entire production, and like usual, it took a half-hour before I'd marginally improved my own looks and was able to finish getting ready and head out.

As I walked out of my bedroom, I could still hear something moving around in her bedroom and took a deep breath. I needed to just confront her. I needed to get this out of the way and not tiptoe around and wonder if my artist best friend roommate was going to snap and do something super weird. And probably artistic.

The door was shut tight, and I was sure it was probably locked like it was earlier today. I knocked a couple of times and waited, wondering if I should be the one running to my room now. I was going to break the bubble.

"Just a second," Star said from somewhere in her room. There was a bit of a commotion in there, like she was moving stuff around, and her voice was slightly muffled.

I waited, wondering what was taking her so long, when finally the door creaked open just an inch. Her face stuck between the door and the frame, the one visible eye rolling until it met mine. She had a grin on her face, from what I could see, but didn't seem to be sweating, and there was no scented candle smell.

"H-hey," I said.

"Hi, Lila," she said, sounding cheerful, but her smile disappeared. Her one visible eye looked panicked now. "Ooh, you look pretty. What's up?"

"I was ... I was just wondering what you're up to in there," I stumbled out, both confused and flattered by the compliment.

"Me?" she asked.

"Yeah. You."

"Oh, you know," she said. "Stuff."

"Stuff?"

"I'm... working on a project," she said, like the idea just came to her.

"Oh," I said. "Cool. Is it for class?"

"No," she said, shaking her head and not dropping her expression at all.

"No?"

"No," she said. "It's… it's just a project. A personal one. Very personal."

"Oh," I said, nodding hesitantly. "Sure. Yeah, that sounds cool. So. I needed to talk to you about something."

"What's up?"

"Can you come out of your room? It's really weird looking at you through the crack of a door."

"I'd rather not," she said, still sounding cheerful. "It's messy in here, and I don't want you to see it. I'd be embarrassed."

"Star, it's fine. I would just like to see your *whole* face."

She sighed.

"Hold on."

The door shut for a brief moment, and when it opened again, she slid herself through the small opening, making sure I didn't see anything in her room. What the hell was she doing in there?

"What's up, roomie?" she asked.

"Okay. Well, first off, thank you."

"You're welcome," she said, a bright smile on her face. I wondered if it was genuine or insane. To be fair, I never really knew the answer to that question, even well before I possibly pissed her off. She wasn't the world's most stable person on the best of days.

"Second, I wanted to talk to you before I headed out again."

"Sure," she said. "Where you going?"

"See, that's the thing," I said. "I'm going over to Gavin's place."

I winced a little, waiting for some kind of reaction. Anything. Yelling, crying, swinging, something. Instead I got a few blinks and that unnervingly cheerful smile.

"Cool," she said finally.

"Cool?" I repeated, then shook my head. "We have to talk about the whole"—I made a complicated motion with my hands that didn't make any sense and yet, she seemed to completely understand—"situation."

"I agree," she said. "You two have a lot to talk about."

Still no real change of expression. I couldn't tell if it was sarcasm, earnestness, or a warning.

"So I might be gone a while. I'll message you before I head back though. I just didn't want you to worry, and I thought you ought to know I was going over there."

"Good," she said. "Have fun!"

With that, the hand that never left the doorknob the entire conversation, turned and opened the door. She slipped inside, never breaking eye contact, and shut the door between us. I stood there a moment, creeped out and unsure of what to do next.

"Okay..." I said to a closed door. "I'll see you later."

The music cut back on as I spoke, but otherwise, there was no response. I backed away, not wanting entirely to turn my back on the door until I was in the living room. I wanted to grab my umbrella in case it opened up, and a cold water bottle from the fridge to stave off the heat and humidity. As I grabbed them, I kept stopping, waiting to hear if she opened the door again. But there was nothing other than the sound of her music playing in the background and the occasional movement in the room. If she was dancing, she was being very careful.

I went to the front door, looking back at her bedroom one more time, and this time, I could hear something beyond the music. A mumbling. Star, talking to herself in a low, hushed tone.

I had heard her do that before too. Back during finals, when she was working on an especially complex and important project. She fretted about it for days before even picking up a brush, and when she did, she talked herself through the entire process before, during, and afterwards. It was like she had to completely guide herself through it.

I couldn't make out what she was saying, but it sounded like the other times she had done this. There was only one major difference. And it was one that was giving me a lot of pause.

She had never, ever, kept any of her art from me. No matter the progress level, no matter the subject matter, nothing. There were times where I wished she *had* kept them from me, and she hadn't, surprising me as I came out of the bathroom or in the middle of eating dinner with a painting of her interpretation of lost souls being tortured or one very revealing painting that was a self-portrait but only of the area between her kneecaps and her navel.

I was no prude, but there were certain parts of your roommate you shouldn't be able to see in artistic but very detailed views. Not if you want to be able to see them the same way again for a while.

Weirded out, I closed the door behind me and tried to shake it off. I needed my brain to be as clear as possible going to Gavin's place. I wanted to make sure that this was a night where we talked. Nothing more. We talked about what had happened and where we were going to go from here.

And maybe I could tell him about how batty Star had been acting. If anything, it might be good news for him. He might have dodged a bullet. A crazy, beautiful, unpredictable bullet.

Chapter Ten

Gavin

CANDLES. WHY DIDN'T I own any candles? And why did Kev have like a million scented ones?

I had been running around frantically searching for candles for a half hour before finally texting Kevin to ask if he had any. I vaguely recalled us having some back last summer when the tornado warnings were going on and wind knocked out the power for a few days. We had little tea lights and some full-size candles to light the apartment and had to run down to the student commons to charge our phones and laptops on a rotating basis.

He didn't even hesitate when I texted him to ask if he had any. Just pointed me to a seldom used shelf in the linen closet, a closet that I only ever used to grab towels for showers and the occasional blanket from the bottom in the winter. Apparently the whole top two shelves were chock full of candle and candle accessories.

I knew Kevin liked to burn them. The house always smelled nice like sandalwood or pine or pumpkin or fresh cotton, whatever the season called for. Now I knew that the reason for it was a giant collection of various scented candles tucked away and labeled on that shelf, along with various holders, votives, and the like. In the box marked 'Generic,' there was a large collection of unscented candles, tealights, and two crystal-looking holders. I pulled all of those out and started lighting them with the dollar store lighter I had bought and barely used three years ago.

I was just about to light the two in the tiny dining room area, in the crystal holders and sitting in the center of our short, rectangular dining room table, when Gavin texted again.

Groaning, I read his text. Not now. I was almost ready, and tonight needed to be perfect.

"Hey Boss," his text read, "Emma has class early tomorrow, so I'm thinking about coming home. Are you still doing that thing tonight?"

It was as specific as I needed it to be. That 'that thing' was me having Lila over to talk about what we were to each other. And hopefully settle on something better than 'someone I used to know.' The candles were part of that. Kevin being there was most certainly not.

"Yes," I responded. "Could I have a few more hours, though?"

"I guess," he typed back. "Can I ask why I can't come home?"

"I'm having Lila over," I texted, rolling my eyes. Kevin being nosy again. "We are going to talk."

What followed were a series of emojis, that when read together provided a rather graphic scene that was incredibly rude, wildly inappropriate, and pretty funny.

"Not like that," I responded. "Just talk."

I heard the phone ding again in my pocket, but by then it was too late. There was a knock on the door. I straightened up too fast and actually hit my head on the low-hanging light above the table. A piece of the glass popped out and only because of my incredible agility and eye-hand coordination was I able to catch it before it broke.

"Just a second," I called out, looking from the glass to the light and back again, overwhelmed and confused. "Now, how the hell..."

I placed the glass in place, and it fell perfectly into its slot.

"It can't be that easy," I muttered, and shook the light. Sure enough, it held its place, and I shrugged. Either I'd gotten lucky or it was going to fall in the middle of dinner, send broken glass into the salads, and kill us both.

If we got as far as the salads before she rolled out.

Checking myself in the mirror above the tiny bar that Kevin brought from home, I took a deep breath. I had never, in my life, been this nervous about talking to a girl before. I was Gavin *Fucking* Freeman. I was the all-star all through high school, the phenom in college. Girls flocked to me. I was cool.

So why the hell was I adjusting the tie and wishing I had parted my hair on the side rather than in the middle like some kind of dork?

Oh well, I thought to myself. *It's not like this is going to go well. Keep your expectations low. She's probably going to come in here, tell me she wants nothing to do with me ever again, and go home. It won't matter if I looked nice or put in effort with the place. She may not even take a step inside.*

Crossing the dining room, I kept repeating in my brain to just be cool. Not to overanalyze. Listen. Let her vent. Be honest and apologetic. But also be firm. I was interested in her. She needed to know that before she left. That I wanted to pursue things with her, if that was something she wanted too. I closed my hand over the knob and turned.

I wasn't prepared for how beautiful she looked.

It had only been a couple of days since I had last seen her, but the vision of her on that beach had been in the forefront of my mind ever since. She was in almost every thought. Even on the mound, I saw a vision of her. Standing just behind home plate. Smiling.

She was wearing makeup, which was unusual for her. She was so pretty without it she didn't need it, but when she did wear it, it only brought out her eyes and her lips even more prominently. I marveled at how I had missed how drop-dead gorgeous she was all this time. Here I had been chasing her roommate, when frankly, to me, Star didn't hold a candle to her.

It helped that she was simply wearing a little sundress. Blues and yellows stood out against her bronze skin, tanned by sunshine. Her blond hair fell down just over her shoulders, and her blue and yellow sneakers matched, giving the effect of a bright blue sky on a warm sunny day. Her bright red lips looked like a candy apple in the center, and I wanted more than I could possibly say to taste them and see if they were as sweet as they looked.

"Hey," she said after a moment.

I realized I had just been standing there, my jaw gently dropping as I looked at her.

"Oh, yeah, hey," I said. "Come in, please."

She smiled. In that smile, I knew this wasn't going to be a bad night. It might not be a great night, but it wouldn't be a bad one. She was at least going to be cordial. She crossed over to halfway between the dining area and the living room, looking around for a moment before turning to me.

"You look like you've rearranged things since I've last been here," she said.

I nodded.

"Sort of. More like just made it look less like an apartment where two college guys live."

She laughed. It was short, truncated by the stress of our current situation I was sure, but a laugh nonetheless. I would take it gladly.

"So I am making dinner. Nothing fancy, just some salads and then pasta. I have the table all set for us, but if you'd like, we can go in the living room and talk for a bit first."

"Sure," she said. "I don't know if I can stay for dinner, but it's very nice of you."

"Of course," I said, feeling a little deflated. "No big deal."

She took the lead, heading into the living room and sitting down on the couch. I sat on the loveseat across from her. For a moment, there was silence as she looked around and I tried to think of how to start.

There probably wasn't a really smooth way to do it. I should just get it out there and deal with the fallout however it happened.

"I like the dragon," she said.

"Star and I are officially over," I said simultaneously.

"What?"

"Huh?"

"What did you say?" she asked.

There was a pause.

"You first," I said.

"I... I was just noticing the dragon. Up there on the TV. That's new, isn't it?"

"Oh," I said, following her gaze. "Yes, it's new. I got it while we were in Myrtle. When the bus couldn't go anywhere for a bit and we were waiting on the backup, I went to the gift shop at the bottom of the hotel."

"There was a gift shop?"

"There's always a gift shop," I said. "But yes, and they had a few little ornaments and knick-knacks. I bought that one."

"He's cute," she said, standing and crossing over to it, picking him up. "I didn't say it said Myrtle Beach on it."

"Yeah, it's a little more subtle than some of the other stuff. It's why I liked it," I said. I cleared my throat. "Um. I, uh, I broke up with Star. Or, well, it's over at any rate. I'll be honest, I don't even know for sure that we ever really were a couple."

I was looking down at the ground.

"Oh?" she said, still holding the dragon and turning it over in her hands.

"Yeah. Like, officially though. Look. I have a text from her."

I pulled out my phone and pulled up the message. I turned it toward her, but she only briefly looked over her shoulder to glance at it. I was a little puzzled. I thought that, no matter what kind of reaction she was going to have to the news, she would at least like to be able to see the evidence first-hand.

That was unless she had already talked to Star, knew about the text and had information that I did not have yet. Information I was sure I was going to get very soon. Potentially unpleasant information.

She nodded.

"I kind of figured," she said.

"You did?" I asked, curious as to what had happened since she came home. Surely she had seen Star. I was deadly curious as to how that interaction went.

"Well, when she didn't mention you at all, and still hasn't, I kind of figured that she was just kind of beyond this whole situation. You know how Star is. If it doesn't interest her, she just ignores it. I kind of get the feeling none of this is interesting to her. So, you know, it's just non-existent to her."

"Oh," I said.

"I tried talking to her about it," she continued. "I gave it a shot. I brought up everything, even mentioned what happened on the beach. She just waved it away. Like it didn't matter. Waved it away and went back to whatever it was she was doing."

"The beach," I said. "You specifically mentioned the beach."

"I did."

"About that..."

"No," she said. It was firm. Firm and pensive at the same time. Like she was assertively telling me 'not right now' rather than a hard 'no.'

"No?"

"No," she repeated. "Not right now. I need some time to think about all this. It's... it's a lot."

"Think about what?" I asked. I swallowed hard. I was about to do something really dumb. Or really smart. But probably really, really dumb. "Lila, I... I think I am falling in love with you."

The silences of before had nothing on this one. This was one of those epic silences, where the brain becomes a time distillation machine, slowing everything down so that you can hear every thump of your heart with seconds between each. Where the background falls out of focus and your eyes water, and all that is clear, the only thing in crystal clear, high definition clarity is the person you are talking to.

I could see her breathing hard. I watched as the color rushed up her neck to her cheeks. How her eyes dilated. Her lips parted.

"What?"

"I know," I said, standing and crossing the room so I could stand a few feet from her.

I could feel heat coming off her body. Heat and tension. It was like I was moving underwater as I walked and when I stopped, I felt like I didn't even need to stand. I could float. I could let go, and my body would be cushioned by the air, so thick it was like a mattress, holding me up in front of her. My temples tingled. The hair on the back of my neck stood up. I licked my lips because they had suddenly gone dry.

"It's stupid," I continued. "But it isn't, is it? You feel it too. We've spent a lot of time together. I know you. I know that when I am around you, I am a different person. A better person. I also know that I want that feeling all of the time. Every day when I wake up, every night when I go to bed, I want that feeling of being the best version of me. A version of me inspired by you. Lila, I want to be with you. Because... I love you."

Chapter Eleven

Lila

I FELT LIKE I COULDN'T breathe.

My vision kept pulsing, the sides bending inward and distorting everything except what was right in the center. Which was Gavin. Standing there with bruises turned nearly black on his face, yet still beautiful. Perhaps even more so, because I'd seen what had created those bruises. I was there for that moment, and we had fought together. I had protected him from having worse happen. I'd watched him get up from blows most other men would crumple from.

Bravery. Intelligence. Tenderness. Thoughtfulness. All traits Gavin had, that I had witnessed with my own eyes. He'd fought off a gang. He'd helped me pass a class I would have surely failed and seemed to ace every subject he came across. He cared for me when I was sick. He checked on me when no one else would have in his position.

He was perfect.

All this time, I had crushed on him but wouldn't let my heart think of it as any more than that. A silly crush. A crush on a man out of my league, who was dating my perfect housemate. A crush that I would relegate to shower fantasies and memories of one stolen kiss by crashing waves that I only got because he was so confused about everything in his life.

Or was he?

Here he was, in his living room, standing feet from me, so close I could feel his breath on my skin, telling me that he *loved* me.

Emotions were flooding me, at war with each other. *How do I respond to that? It's an impossible situation.*

Then the spell was broken. He stepped forward, and it was like he walked through a waterfall. His eyes entranced me, and the rest of the world fell away. My hands rose as if they were floating, and I realized it was because he had them in his, picking them up and pressing them to his chest. He winced slightly, a memory of the pain in his shoulder, but his eyes never left mine. Intense. Burning.

I couldn't hold it back anymore. The thoughts, the fears, the worries, all bundled up like snakes in a ceramic bowl, snipping at each other, fighting to be the first one to exit. I didn't feel like I had control of my lips. They were numb anyway. They were going to say what the heart felt, because the brain had checked out, abdicating responsibility for the first time in my memory.

It was with my heart that I spoke.

"I think I love you too."

My eyes widened as I heard my voice say those words. I couldn't believe they were there, but they were, inescapable and real, thudding into the air like hammers. What was said could not be unsaid. Not for anyone's sake. Not Star's. Not Gavin's. Not my own. They were there because they were *real.*

"Yeah?" he asked, a grin curling up one side of his lips.

I nodded, the same smile taking over my own.

"Yeah."

"Yeah."

"I love you."

The last words were nearly cut off as I took in a deep breath and he dipped his head to kiss me. As our lips touched, an explosion of color and heat and reality smacked over me, warming me from the top of my head down to my toes. Like an egg cracking and the yolk dripping down, I was covered in it, and it made me feel like I could melt right then and there.

So I did.

His arms wrapped around me, and I sank into them, letting him hold me aloft as he kissed me. His tongue slid into my mouth and danced with mine, and I tasted him. It tasted like ecstasy.

Suddenly, his hands slid down to my ass and picked me up. It was just as well. My knees didn't work anymore anyway. He carried me for a moment as I curled into his massive arms. I felt weightless, delicate, probably for the first time since I was a tiny child. Then his lips broke from mine, and his eyes stared meaningfully into my own.

"If you feel uncomfortable at any time—" he began.

I pressed my lips to his again, stopping him. The message was clear. I didn't want to stop either.

I giggled as he kicked the door of his bedroom open and then slammed it shut with the other foot. He carried me to the bed and gently laid me down on it, crawling on below my waist and pushing apart my thighs. I let my hands fall back behind my head as he gently pushed the hem of my dress up a few inches and kissed my knees first, then slowly slid up the insides of my leg.

Gasping, I reached down to fill my hand with his dark hair, and he ran his tongue back down me, then up again, inching higher toward my center. The dress moved up and up until my black panties were exposed and his tongue was tantalizingly close to the edge of the fabric. I wanted to reach down and tear them off, but Gavin was in control. He was moving around my body like a man possessed, a man worshiping, enjoying every single second.

Suddenly, he stopped, sitting up and undoing his tie. I moaned as he ripped it off and unbuttoned the buttons of his shirt slowly, his eyes never leaving mine. As he pulled the shirt off, exposing a chest and stomach covered in muscles and bruises, I reached out for him and ran my fingers down him. He leaned forward again, pressing his lips into mine, and I slid my hand down his stomach and under his pants.

I was desperate for him. I needed him, like I had wanted him that night on the beach but a million times stronger. I was a slave to the desire. My fingertips brushed through the silky strands of hair at his core and then stopped at the ridged, veiny, warm skin of his cock. I groaned. So did he.

Reaching down, he unbuckled his belt with one hand and then undid the clasp of his slacks. Continuing to pull, the zipper lowered, and I realized he wasn't wearing boxers underneath. The tuft of black hair revealed itself, and soon my hand was no longer bound by the pressure of his pants. I let myself stroke him, and the sound both of our bodies made was one of intense carnal joy.

His cock was long, thick, and warm. I suddenly felt desperate to have it in my mouth, and I scooted down a few inches. He grinned as he positioned himself, knees on either side of my chest. I couldn't wipe the expectant, devious grin from my face as I brought his member to my lips and slid out my tongue. I ran it up along the undershaft, relishing in the way his body tensed and moaned before I reached the head and swirled around it, gathering up the sweet juices that lay there and plunging him into my mouth.

He was so long, so thick, that I couldn't fit him all in my mouth. The head slid across my tongue and into my throat as I stroked him into me and then pulled him out, wet and throbbing now. I stroked him as I watched him open his eyes again and look down at me. I felt incredible in that gaze. It was one of intense pleasure, of desire, of worship. I took him into my mouth again, and he rocked gently.

I closed my eyes as I bobbed back and forth, relishing in taking him deep into my mouth and squeezing my lips over his cock. But they opened when I felt his fingers slide under my panties. I looked up to see him curling over backwards. He rearranged himself so both knees were on one side and then he lay down beside me. Kicking off his pants, he settled by pulling me on top of him with my legs straddling his head.

My panties fell to my knees, and I had to take him out of my lips to moan deeply as I felt his tongue slide between my lower lips and onto my clit. It was like he knew my body already, and every touch was following an erotic roadmap. I cried out as the tip of his tongue brushed over and swirled around my clit, encouraging the hood to open and the rest of my body to freeze and clench. I buried my face in his thigh, slowly stroking his cock against my cheek as he licked me, increasing in speed and intensity.

I could feel a climax coming already. His touch was gentle but firm, knowing and yet exploratory. I took in a deep, hitching breath as the feeling washed over me. My hips were moving in spite of themselves as I rocked over his face. One hand had slid up my thigh and now a finger penetrated me, entering me and sending me into another, higher form or orgasm. As the pad of his finger brushed over my upper wall and his tongue continued to stimulate my clit, I could hold on no more. I cried out as the climax washed over me.

My toes curled. My breath escaped me in a wild cry. I stuffed my mouth with his cock to silence me, to take him inside me, to pleasure him. I gagged as it hit the back of my throat, and his free hand reached down to push on the back of my neck, encouraging me to go further.

I vibrated and shook, uncontrollable orgasms rattling my body. The room spun as I felt myself flung onto my back, the sudden warmth of his body missing as he repositioned himself. Then his hands grabbed at my ankles and slid me toward him forcefully, and yet with a tenderness of touch. He wouldn't hurt me.

Not unless I asked him to.

He settled between my thighs just as I started to gain control of my breathing again. It was as if my mind forced itself to settle so it didn't miss a moment of this. This monumental, fantastical few seconds when he would enter me for the first time. I needed to be ready. I wanted to keep this memory forever.

His upper thighs, just above the knees, settled against the bottoms of mine. I reached down to stroke him against me, pushing the head down into my wet pussy to gather the juices there and make him even slicker than my mouth had been able to do. He hovered over me, fists pushing down into the mattress on either side of me and pressing.

His thick, long, massive cock penetrated me, and I cried out in a mixture of pure intense joy and a pressure-filled pain. He was so big it felt like he was stretching me, and yet, I wanted him in deeper. I wanted to mold myself around him. To let him get so deep inside me that he claimed me for his own.

Grunting with sweat and sex, he slowly rocked back and then forward again, over and over as he drove his cock deeper inside me. For a moment, I saw stars, my body unable to breathe or think or function at all. I was vibrating, rolling through an extended, incredible, life-altering climax as I felt him drive deeper inside me.

Then he held himself there inside me, our bodies as close as two bodies could be, my feet, still clenching and curling and shaking, wrapped around his legs, like I was begging him to stay. His eyes bore into mine, and I watched as they ran through emotions. I reached up to kiss him, and he rocked back harder. I groaned between the embraces and then lay back, pulling the dress up and over my head. My breasts tumbled out, and I watched his eyes fall down to them before he dove his face into the center of my chest.

As his body rocked into me, he took one nipple into his lips and sucked, his tongue flicking the taut, sensitive peak and driving me even more wild than I already was. Adrenaline was filling me and a desire for another, even more intense climax was building, yearning, demanding release. I clenched my hands around him, pulling him tight as my eyes opened wide and met his.

"Fuck me, Gavin," I groaned.

His eyes darkened, and his grin widened. I watched as his muscles flexed and his body tightened. He began to slam into me with force, with speed, with a needful desire. Our foreheads pressed together as we stared into each other's eyes. Our bodies made noises, deep, carnal noises as he rammed into me over and over. I could feel the moment coming. He was near climax. So was I. We just had to let go.

I leaned back, arching my back, pressing my breasts up into his face as he curled his hands around my back, lifting my ass as he thundered into me. A mighty roar built in his chest. I matched it with a wail of my own.

Then he came. I came with him. Hot, pulsing, gushing, we climaxed together and fell together in exhaustion when we were done. My body tingled, and I felt like I might pass out as he rolled over onto his back and pulled me into his chest. Breathless, I kissed his neck and settled into the crook of his arm.

The last thing I remembered was his lips pressing into the top of my head.

Chapter Twelve

Gavin

THE FRONT DOOR OPENED in the living room and shut, waking me up.

I had been tuned to notice that all my life. Growing up with my parents, it wasn't uncommon for doors to open in the middle of the night, but I had to be alert about it. Sometimes it meant Mom had come home from Ladies' Night, or Dad had wandered back from the biker bar or had returned from a prize fight he probably lost. But sometimes it meant someone else was in the place, stealing whatever looked valuable so they could buy more meth or get back at Dad for something he did.

I learned to keep all my valuables in my bed with me. Underneath my bed as a kid was everything I held dear. My video game system, the eight-pack of expensive drawing markers I'd gotten for Christmas that I was pretty sure Dad stole from the craft store he took a part time job at that winter, my Cubs hat with the silver Maddux signature on the bill, and my backpack. The backpack was where my books for school were, sure, but it also had two sheets of plastic card protectors with my most valuable baseball cards. Cards that I now had in my dresser, one of which was signed. It was my goal in life to get them all signed.

But I wasn't a kid anymore, and I wasn't at my parents' house. If I could help it, I would never step foot in any place they called home ever again.

I was at my apartment I shared with Kevin, in my own room, curled up in bed with Lila.

Because *that happened.*

I could barely believe it. Somehow, I had turned a night I was positive was going to end in her going home early and me doing everything I could to angle for her to at least speak to me again someday, into a night of the greatest experience of my life. I had thrown no-hitters, I had hit grand slams, I had won scholarships and walked-off championship games with deep fly balls to the corner outfield stands. None of it compared to spending the night with Lila.

There was such an intense connection between us, something so much more raw and deep than just sex, it was like religion. Or how I'd had religion explained to me anyway. My parents never really did much with religion, other than steal from a collection plate once. And use charities to pay off bills they got behind on.

I turned to look at the alarm clock on my nightstand. It was ancient, and I should probably just chuck it, since everyone I knew used their phone for an alarm these days. But I felt nostalgic for it. It was an old speaker one and had been with me since I was nine and Dad brought it home from some thrift store. It had still been in its package, and I had been needing an alarm clock. The reason for needing one, of course, was that I had almost failed school because my parents weren't waking me up early enough to catch the bus. If I didn't want to repeat fifth grade, I was going to have to start doing that myself.

Now it was showing just after midnight in its green digital numbers, the dot representing that an alarm was set for the morning hanging high above the time.

Just after midnight, and the door was opening, but I wasn't going anywhere. It was just Kevin. I had my door shut and the little box fan going nearby. He would be able to hear that and know my sleeping ritual had begun.

I listened, my eyes drooping shut as he made his way down the hallway to his room. It was a familiar enough routine. Kevin liked to stay out sometimes, and I was usually already asleep when he came home. He knew how to be quiet, and I gave him a little leeway since he was a literal giant and it was hard to be quiet when you were Fee Fi Fo Fumming it in the middle of the night.

Then, to my surprise, I heard something else. Something decidedly *not* Kevin. Another voice, as a point of fact.

The thing was, Kevin *never* brought people home. It just wasn't his thing. He had his space, and it was sacred. He might bring them to the apartment to hang out in the living room, but they wouldn't go to his bedroom. It was a rule. One I had never seen or heard of him breaking.

Yet, I could hear the door creak open across from my own, Kevin shushing and the sound of Emma, unmistakably Emma, giggling as she followed him inside. Then the door shut and locked, and silence took back over the night. I smiled to myself.

Good for Kevin.

Good for Emma.

As Lila turned in her sleep, curling her back into my chest and pulling my hand over her to wrap around and gently lay over her breast, I smiled wider.

Good for me.

I drifted back to sleep the happiest I had been in my entire life.

In a first, I was awoken by someone nibbling my ear. I opened my eyes and caught sight of one of Lila's naked breasts, poking up out of the sheet and brushing against my ribs. Instantly, my cock hardened, and I turned my head toward her. She giggled in surprise, and I pulled her tightly into me for a kiss.

It was a sweet kiss, one of passion and joy but also playfulness. When we released each other's lips, she kissed down my chin, to my neck, to my chest and then to my sternum.

"Careful now," I said.

"Or else?" she teased playfully.

"Or else," I said, reaching down and grabbing her waist to the sound of her playful laughter. I pulled her up onto my stomach, and she stretched out over me, wiggling her body down until her hot core was just over my thick, standing member.

"Someone is awake already," she said.

"Perhaps we should help him get back to sleep."

"How do we do that?" she said, blinking her eyes innocently.

I laughed, pulling her back down to me for a kiss again as I reached down below her ass. I pushed on the bottom of my cock until it found the opening of her and slid just the slightest bit inside.

"Like that," I groaned.

She closed her eyes and sank down on me, and I could feel how wet she was already. I was more than ready for another round myself, and as she sat up, I put my hands on her hips to guide her and took in the vision of her naked body grinding on mine.

"Oh, like this?" she asked, beginning to bounce a bit.

"You've got it," I groaned.

She leaned forward, rocking slowly as she reached for the headboard for stability. I filled my hand with her ass and the other with one of her breasts as I took the other into my mouth. She moaned deeply, and it was at that moment I remembered Kevin coming in the night before. I looked up, catching her eyes and put one finger over my lips.

"Shhh," I said.

"Why?" she asked.

"Kevin came home last night," I said. "He brought Emma."

"Oh," she said, her eyes going wide and suddenly shrinking down on me. "You don't think they heard me, do you?"

"No, no, not at all," I half lied. The walls in this place weren't exactly thick. But at the same time, Kevin was a deep sleeper.

"Wait. Oh shit."

"What?"

"What time is it?"

I turned my head to look at the alarm clock, the alarm still yet to go off.

"Nine," I said. "Wow. We slept la—"

"OH SHIT!"

Lila hopped up off of me, and the sudden coolness of the air on my wet, hardened cock sent a chill up me.

"What's the matter?" I asked.

"I'm late for class," she said, rolling off the bed and digging through the clothes crumpled on the floor.

"Oh, damn," I said. "Okay, hang on. I think your panties are over here."

I crossed the room to where I remembered flinging her underwear as she put her dress back on. Her nipples were still taut, and the effect was almost as erotic as seeing her topless. Her hardened nipples poking through the thin blue and yellow fabric, knowing that they would be like that for a while and the reason was because we were in bed together, was enough to make me want to bend her over and pull up the dress again right now, damn the class.

"There they are," she said, pointing to a spot just beyond my feet. "Toss them here."

I did as she asked, though reluctantly, then crossed over to my dresser. I opened a drawer and pulled out a T-shirt and a pair of light sweatpants. Tossing them on, I went to her, embracing her with a deep kiss.

"You ready?" I asked.

"No," she said. "I have to do the walk of shame."

"I'm sure they're still asleep," I said. "Kev likes to sleep in when he can."

"I hope so," she said.

"We can get you out of here and back to your place and no one will know," I said.

"Star will."

I shrugged.

"I guess so."

"That will be a fun conversation," she muttered.

"Look, we can get you out of here, get a quick kiss on the way, and then you can change and head to class. We can meet later for breakfast and coffee, okay?"

"Okay," she said. "Breakfast sounds amazing. I kind of worked up an appetite."

I grinned. "I wonder how you did that."

"I wonder," she said, smiling.

Reaching up on her toes, she pressed her lips to mine again.

"I wish you didn't have to go," I said. "I wasn't done with you yet."

"Neither was I," she said. "But I can't miss this class. Not all of it anyway. I don't have anyone to get notes from."

"All right then," I said. "We slip out. We kiss. You run to your place. I shower and get changed and then we meet at Lucky's for breakfast? Or you can come back here, and I can make something."

"You cook?"

"Poorly," I said. "I mean, I can make breakfast. I can make a handful of meals. I actually made stuff for us... last... night. Oh no."

"Oh no?"

"I might have left everything out on the counter. Which means Kevin saw it. Hopefully he didn't eat everything, but he would have certainly seen I was planning on having someone over."

"The candles probably gave you away," she said. "Nice touch, by the way."

"I thought so," I said. "Okay, so Kevin will have known you came by and stayed. No biggie, right? You just come back over here for breakfast, we tell him officially, and then we go from there."

"To where?" she asked.

"To... the future," I said, lamely.

She grinned. "I like that," she said. "Our future."

"Our future," I agreed.

She took a deep breath and shook her head and arms as she exhaled.

"Okay. Let's do it."

"All right," I said, nodding affirmatively. Then I clasped the doorknob, unlocked it, and opened it quietly. We made it a few steps down the hall before I stopped in my tracks. Lila ran into me from behind and then realized why.

"Fuck," Lila said behind me in a whispered curse.

"Oh, hey, guys!"

"Emma?" I asked, my brain going quickly and trying to project the shame before it could be applied on us.

Emma was standing in the living room, wearing one of Kevin's T-shirts, which was comically big on her. It went all the way down to her kneecaps, and the neckline dipped between her breasts. She was grinning like a lunatic and holding two mugs that had tendrils of steam rising from them. The room smelled like fresh coffee.

"Hey," Kevin said, poking his head into the hallway from the kitchen. He was mixing something yellow in a bowl. He was also grinning like a lunatic, and his eyes flickered between me and Lila, though not with a hint of surprise or judgment. "Want some breakfast? I'm about to throw on some eggs and bacon. Morning, Lila."

"Hi," I heard her say behind me and then her head pressed into the center of my chest. "So much for the plan," she whispered.

Chapter Thirteen

Lila

THIS JUST KEPT GETTING better and better and better.

Of course, I didn't regret anything I did last night. Quite the opposite, in fact. I was absolutely thrilled with how the night had gone. But since realizing I was already running late to my class, things had just continually gone downhill. It was all made worse by the fact that I simply wanted to say fuck it all, grab Gavin, go back to his room, have him screw my brains out again and then do absolutely nothing but be naked and have orgasms for the rest of the week.

I felt like that was a solid plan.

Unfortunately, I *needed* to go to class. And I would have to address this whole situation with Star rather soon, too. As much as I didn't want to.

That was if Emma didn't spoil it for me, that was.

"*Good morning,* Lila," Emma said, with as much sass and meaning as her tiny, diminutive body could accomplish.

For a split second, my brain trailed away and actually tried to imagine how the two of them could have sex. She was so tiny, and he was so giant. It couldn't be comfortable.

Then I shuddered and tried to block that thought from ever appearing in my mind again.

"Good morning, Emma," I said.

I smiled as best I could and tried to slip by her. She was coming down the hallway, turning sideways to get by us while carrying her coffee. I turned as well, and kept my eyes on the mugs, hoping they didn't spill out. When we reached the end of the hallway, Kevin was smiling, holding a spatula and looking rather pleased with himself.

"If you guys don't want anything, I'm going to shut this on down," he said.

"It's fine," Gavin said. "We're going to go out for brunch. She's late for class."

"Ahh," Kevin said. "Well, have a good day."

Whistling a jaunty little tune, he picked up the two plates of eggs, bacon, and toast and carried them down the hall after Emma. When the door shut, Lila groaned and rolled her eyes.

"What the hell is she doing here?" I whisper-yelled.

"She came in last night with Kevin," he said. "I heard them come in around midnight."

"Why didn't you tell me?" I asked.

"You were asleep! On top of me!"

I felt my face flush. In spite of myself, I was smiling.

"I would have liked to have known!"

"Sorry."

"Now everyone will know!"

Gavin cocked his head to the side and raised an eyebrow.

"Is that a problem?"

I stammered for a moment, unable to respond. I could feel my jaw flapping up and down, but no sound was coming out of it. Gavin grinned and brushed by me, opening the door and turning back around. I was just starting to form sound in my throat when he pulled me tight for a kiss, and I sank into it.

He held me there in that moment, and I didn't want to leave. I was almost willing to throw it all away just to go back down to that bedroom again. But I had to steel myself. I let my hand run down his chest and over his soft sweatpants. His cock was still thick underneath, and I wondered how obvious it had been when they saw him. I squeezed him, and he moaned into my kiss.

"I'll text you," I whispered into his ear when I broke the embrace.

"Have fun," he said. "Still on for brunch?"

"Maybe," I said, turning around to get one last look at him as I headed down the hall. "I'll let you know."

"Okay," he said, shutting the door.

As I turned back toward the exit of the apartment door, I felt a little cheer developing in my chest. I couldn't believe that had happened. I had slept with Gavin Freeman. What's more, I was now, for all intents and purposes, in a *relationship* with Gavin Freeman. We hadn't talked about that specifically, but you didn't start throwing out 'I love yous' and then having sex immediately after with someone you were just casually seeing.

And it had been *good* sex too. Mind-bending. Earth-shattering. My body was still buzzing from it, though the false start of the morning session didn't help matters in that regard. I almost wished I hadn't even noticed the time. If I had just plain forgotten about it, I would feel better about missing it. But once I remembered, I couldn't just skip it. I had to go.

It was already hot outside, even though it was early, so at least I wasn't cold in the sundress. That was something else to be grateful for. As I pounded down the street, picking up speed as I headed toward my apartment, I decided to just write off the inconvenience of being late to class as part of the hazards of being in a relationship.

Even just thinking about that word made me grin. I had a boyfriend. Not just any boyfriend, but Gavin Freaking Freeman. Literally, the hottest man I had ever seen. The most talented baseball player I had ever seen live. And someone who I considered a dear friend who I could talk to about anything and had often enjoyed just hanging out with. All the questions about compatibility were already answered. I knew I could be with Gavin. We had essentially been together for months; we just didn't know it yet.

He was technically dating Star during that time.

Star who was my roommate.

Star who, likely, was at home right now and was going to see me coming in wearing the same sundress I had been wearing the night before when I was going over to Gavin's not forty-eight hours after she had broken up with him.

If there was a girl code, I'd broken it. I'd shattered it into a million pieces, put some of them onto a rocket, and sent it to the moon.

I had to figure out what I was going to say to Star. She deserved me sitting her down and explaining what was going on and seeing if she had a problem with it. I wasn't going to change what I was doing if she did, but I was going to do what I could to mitigate the problem between us. The fact was, I was madly in love with Gavin. I had been fighting it for months.

If Star had a problem with that, and she very well could, then it might mean we have to separate as roommates. Maybe even friends for a while. The thing was, I loved Star. She was my friend. Probably my best friend. But if I had to choose between my friend and a person that I could very realistically see being happy with for the rest of my life, I would have to pick him. Eventually, Star would find her person too, whoever they might be. I wasn't going to throw away my chance at love with the most perfect specimen ever put on this Earth because it might hurt Star's feelings.

Especially after how she'd treated him.

That was another thing. It wasn't just his story about how Star had acted to him. I was a witness. As much as I wanted to side with my friend, I'd seen her treat him like an afterthought. It wasn't her fault, really, but it was who she was. She was Star. She didn't pay attention to other people the way the rest of us did. She did her own thing, in her own time, with whoever happened to be around her at that moment.

I knew Gavin thought he wanted to be that person, but I wasn't sure any one person could fill that role for Star. She had to have multiple people, at different times in different settings who could fill that role. Because Star was so flighty, so artistically inclined, so rebellious of social norms, she wasn't capable of settling down with any one person. And asking her to was being cruel.

As I thundered up the steps toward our apartment, I went over a few opening lines. None of them sounded decent, but I had to start with something. Just stumbling in and announcing loudly that I had just come back from banging her ex-boyfriend probably was not going to be the best approach. I needed to be somewhat delicate. Star was delicate. In a weird way.

And yet in other ways, she was the most independent, fierce, fearless person I knew.

I climbed the last step, suddenly wondering just what in the hell was going on, anyway. Gavin was dating Star. The most interesting person I knew or had ever known. And he left her to date me, a king-size girl athlete who played softball and rarely wore makeup. Maybe when he had that fight in the parking lot, he got his head hit really hard. One day he'd just wake up and wonder what he had done.

If I could feel good about myself for more than five minutes, it would be great.

I reached the door, pulling out my key and sticking it in the lock before pausing. Maybe I should knock. Give her a moment to prepare herself. I could pretend I forgot my key.

No, that would just remind her that I had been gone all night and didn't even take my key with me. It would mean that I had every intention of spending the night at Gavin's despite telling her I was going over to talk. No, lying wasn't the right call. But knocking might be.

I rapped on the door with three knocks and waited for a moment. The other side of the door sounded awfully quiet. I knew Star had an afternoon class today and usually was up by now, showered, dressed, and either painting or drawing in her sketchpad. I knocked again. Still nothing.

Shrugging, I turned the key and opened the door.

Star was not inside.

Pursing my lips on one side, I walked deeper into the apartment and looked around. Everything looked normal. The couch had one of the blankets strewn across it, the way Star normally did when she got up from drawing. The sketch pad that she always used to doodle with when she was at home was sitting on the coffee table, a pencil and eraser on top of it. A glass of water was next to it, also indicating she had been sitting there recently. She was terrible about putting away dishes.

I made my way down the hall toward our rooms. When I reached hers, I stopped, cupping my ear and putting it on the door. I listened for a moment.

Nothing. Silence. Not even the sound of an oversleeping Star snoring or the sound of music coming from earbuds while she lay on the bed and did whatever weird meditation she did before she painted. Or the sounds of her exercising, doing yoga and stretching and contorting into positions I was sure made her even *more* popular among the boys that saw her do it when she went to the park with her mat.

She was gone.

I turned toward my door and stopped as I reached it. I was already reaching for the linen closet to grab towels when my eyes fell on the sticky note on my door. It was one of the blue ones, which I knew were her favorites. She used those exclusively to leave me notes or herself notes about happy things. If it were chores or bills or something, it was the red ones. Star liked to color-code her life.

On the blue note, her careful, yet light and free handwriting spelled out a message for me. I read it in mild confusion.

"Seems like I missed you this morning.

Or last night.

See you later."

There was a heart underneath with a star inside it, a signature she had used ever since I had known her at least. Then below that was more writing.

"Oh, your coach came by. Seemed very excited. Wants you to come by her office ASAP."

My eyebrow cocked, and I sat back on my heels. What would Coach want? And why didn't she just text me?

I pulled out my phone from my pocket and immediately realized the problem. My phone was dead. Groaning, I slipped it back into my pocket and tore the note off the door, taking it with me inside. I needed to change and bird bath shower and get the hell out of there. As it was, I was going to miss the first fifteen minutes of class, and then have to book it over to Coach's office.

But as I hopped in the shower to clean up and get dressed, my mind went back to the first half of the note.

"Or last night.

See you later."

That had to be catty, right? She noticed I wasn't there. And she was being kind of catty about it.

It made me mad, but I had to remember, I needed to afford her room to be upset.

I just didn't have to let it affect me.

Chapter Fourteen

Gavin

AS I SHUT THE DOOR and turned around, the sound of Kevin's door opening got my attention. No one came out of it immediately, so I headed into the kitchen. There were a couple pieces of bacon sitting there, and while I was thinking about meeting her for brunch, she wasn't entirely sure it was happening. And I needed to eat.

Figuring I could eat light for brunch, I pulled out the salads that I had already made last night and that Kevin had apparently put away and crunched up the bacon slices over top of them. As I mixed them in and added a drizzle of oil, a face appeared in the kitchen doorframe and startled me.

"Sorry," Emma said as I took a step back and then shook my head.

"It's all right," I said. "I'm just not all the way awake yet."

"Oh trust me, I understand," she said. "I don't get much sleep when I'm with Kevin either."

I really didn't need to hear that, but I was going to let it go out of awkwardness. So instead of groaning and frowning, I faked a laugh and continued mixing up my salad.

"Did Lila leave?" she asked.

"Yeah, she had to head to class," I said.

"Oh, damn," she said. "I was going to make a big breakfast spread for you guys. Kevin and I already had a round of it, but I think we were going to come back for more."

I froze, hands still full of bits of bacon.

"Oh, I thought you guys were done. I kinda used the last of the bacon."

"That's fine," she said, grinning. "Kevin could stand to do with less bacon anyway."

I huffed a laugh again. These two had been together a matter of days, and she was already modifying his diet?

"Yeah, well, good luck with that," I said.

"Oh, crap, I forgot to tell her. Coach texted me this morning. She wants to see Lila as soon as she can."

"What?"

"Coach, she texted me this morning. She said she tried to find Lila and couldn't get in touch with her. Said her phone went right to voicemail."

"Oh," I said. "Well, that's unfortunate."

"It sure is, especially since the meeting is just her and two other girls, of which I am one."

"Oh?" I asked, pulling out a mug and filling it with the coffee that they had made. At least this breakfast was coming together with minimal effort.

"Yeah." She beamed. "She wouldn't say what it was, saying she just wanted to see us, but I think I know what it is."

"You do?" I asked, sitting at the table and taking a giant bite of the salad. I might not be able to cook all that well, but I could make a damn good sandwich and a really fine salad.

"Yup," she said. "We're supposed to meet at one, and I have a one-thirty class, but I'll probably just skip it for this. I'm acing that class anyway."

"That makes sense. So what do you think the meeting is about?"

"Promise you won't say anything?"

"Sure," I said. "Who am I going to tell? Lila's phone's dead."

"Good point," she said, then crossed the kitchen to where I sat, clutching a piece of toast in one hand and a newly refilled mug of coffee in the other. "I think we got scouted."

"Really?" I asked.

"Yup." She nodded. "Lila especially. I mean, I was good this last weekend, but Lila was phenomenal. If anyone was getting scouted, it would probably be her."

"Wow," I said. "I look forward to hearing what she has to say later."

"For sure," she said. "Well, if you're not going to be hungry after that, I guess the rest of the eggs and stuff are free game?"

"Go for it," I said. "I appreciate you guys making them at all."

"No problem," she said, beaming and turning around, heading back down the hall wearing Kevin's shirt like a dress.

I finished my salad in silence, then put away the dish and filled another mug of coffee before going back to my room.

If Lila got scouted, that meant huge things for her. Monumentally huge things. I was incredibly happy for her, but at the same time, I couldn't help but also feel just the slightest bit of jealousy. I was so sure I was going to have a meeting like that of my very own before I hurt my shoulder. Now Lila was looking like she was going to become a huge star and maybe play professionally. Maybe even Olympic teams.

Good for her.

I had to let go of the disappointment in my own performance last weekend. I couldn't help it. I'd gotten my ass kicked. My shoulder was still sore as hell, though it felt a million times better. A couple of weeks and I would be good as new. Or so I hoped.

I sipped my coffee and turned on the tablet I kept in my room. Putting on sports highlights, I went about cleaning up the room a bit. The truth was, I hadn't really done much cleaning in there the day before because I had convinced myself it wouldn't see any action. But now that Lila had not only spent the night in here, but it looked like a repeat performance was likely, I needed to get the place in order.

A basket of clothes I had yet to fold and put away from days ago was first on the list after making the bed. Then I picked up all the trash and tossed it and then went into the bathroom. A quick clean of everything but the shower, and I was ready to get clean myself. I had class at one myself. It wasn't far from where the coaches' offices were, so I was hoping to run into her after my class.

I hopped in the shower and rinsed off, debating with myself if I wanted to let the memories of the night before take over or if I wanted to hold off until I saw her in the flesh again. The delayed satisfaction won out, and I cleaned myself and got dressed for class without resorting to that, despite the fact that my cock was still hard from when she climbed on top of me.

The class was across campus on the side where the ballfields were. Usually, I could cut across main street, through a few sidewalks and be there in ten minutes, but there was some construction blocking my way. It had begun, apparently, while we were in Myrtle Beach and threatened to be going on for a few more weeks, tearing up the road and demolishing a building to build yet another dorm.

Breyer University was enjoying their fame. Part of that, I knew, was me.

Maybe some of it soon would be Lila, too.

I followed the next closest route to my class, watching the time tick away on my phone. As it was, I was going to get there with just enough time to spare to get out my notes and do a quick once-over before class. That professor had a tendency to do surprise quizzes. I liked being ready for them when they dropped. He *hated* that. I got the impression that he desperately wanted to fail the athletes, all because of some purity test about education he was performing for himself.

I didn't care much, but it meant Kevin got poor grades in that class. He ended up dropping it and replacing it with a similar class with a different instructor. I probably should have gone with him, but it was a matter of pride now. I wanted to defeat him by always getting As. I enjoyed the sour look on his face when he saw my papers.

I was nearly to the building when my phone alerted. I stopped, pulling it out of my back pocket and swiping it open. The notification was from Lila, and I opened it eagerly.

"Hey," she typed, "I might be late to brunch. Perhaps we should do dinner? Or just eat at your place? I have a meeting with Coach at one, one-thirty. I'll call you after it's over, and we can make plans then, okay?"

I sent back a smiley face and a thumbs up emoji and stuffed the phone back into my pocket.

I was happy for her. If it was what Emma thought it was, then it was going to be a very good day. I looked forward to celebrating with her. After the performance I heard she put on last weekend, she deserved the recognition. She was a star.

Hah.

I'd traded in a Star for a star.

I probably should keep that joke to myself.

Picking up my speed, I headed for class, rounding the corner and making great time, I dashed to the side door. It was more accessible than the front door and didn't often have a crowd of kids trying to get in or out. It led directly to the stairwell rather than the elevator, and as an athlete, I preferred the stars anyway.

I was grinning. Life was good. I couldn't wait to talk to Lila in a bit and find out for sure what Coach wanted. Nothing could knock me down.

Except...

I froze where I was. My eyes had to be lying to me. I had been very, *very* clear with her. She had absolutely no right to be there, and the look on her face told me what I needed to know. The rest of the day was going to be shot. I was going to have to deal with her bullshit.

My mother was standing by the door to my next class. She had a coffee in one hand and her arms crossed over her chest. She was looking back and forth over the courtyard, but it was only a matter of moments before she saw me. I seriously contemplated turning around and walking the other way. But it was too late. She saw me. She waved.

"Dammit."

Chapter Fifteen

Lila

COACH SAM WAS THE HEAD coach of the team and one of the most enigmatic people I knew. She alternately liked to wear overalls and boots and a ballcap and stomp around campus like she was going to leave early to go take care of the farm, while also sometimes showing up randomly in a pretty dress, fantastic makeup, and her hair blown out so she looked like a very convincing Marilyn Monroe impersonator.

Today, she had chosen the red lipstick and the pink dress. I wondered if there was any connection to good news and dresses, but then I remembered she told me she'd gotten engaged the day before while wearing a cargo shorts, combat boots and a T-shirt that read *Death to the Patriarchy.*

She was sitting in her office, typing on her laptop when I rapped on the door and let myself in. Two other girls, Havana and Grace, were sitting in the office as well, and I kind of figured that the news was going to be good right then. Havana had had a breakout season this year so far, and at six-two and lean, was an incredible physical specimen. She also played like eight other sports, and we knew she was a lock for national teams in some of them. Grace was about my height, but very sturdy and our resident slugger. She hit forth in the lineup and set the school record for home runs last year. She beat me by four and was currently leading me by six this season.

"Hey, guys," I said as I sat down. "Sorry if I'm late."

"You're not late," Coach Sam said, using her mouse to hit something on her screen and then shutting the lid. "Grace, Havana, if you could keep this to yourselves until tonight, I would appreciate it. I want to make a big announcement."

"Sure, Coach," Grace said.

Havana simply nodded, and I noticed she was wearing the biggest smile I had ever seen on her. Her eyes were watery, and she had a look of incredible joy plastered across her face. It was enough to make you want to get emotional for her, especially considering how much of an absolute sweetheart she was.

As they left, I watched Coach Sam pull out a manilla envelope from her desk and start laying out papers so she could see each one. I was curious but didn't want to pry. She kept silent until the girls were gone and the door shut behind them.

"So..." I said.

"Lila," she said, sighing. "Lila, Lila, Lila. You were *fantastic* last weekend."

"Thanks," I said, grinning. "I thought I did pretty well."

"I think everyone will agree you led us to that championship win," she said. "Your performance both on the mound and at the plate was spectacular. So much so that I would have been beside myself if I *didn't* hear about you from scouts at the game."

"There were scouts at the game?" I asked.

She nodded, her lips pursed tight in a grin that looked like it wanted to explode into a wide smile. She was trying to keep her cool, to spread it all out in some dramatic way. Maybe that was the key to the dresses. Maybe she was an actress underneath it all and loved to dress up to play a role when she had something with enough drama to perform.

"Not just scouts, but Olympic scouts. And they were impressed by you."

"Really?" I asked, my chest tightening. "What did they say?"

"Well, so, how this all works with them is they need to see you play on a national team, okay? Something that tours and plays other national teams in exhibition and league play. Then, from the national teams, they invite people to try out for the Olympic team. So the offer is being extended for you to join the southeast national team this summer in an effort to see if you could join the Olympic team in the fall and possibly compete next summer."

"What about my studies?" I asked. "I can't just off and play for some national team and try out for Olympics without missing classes."

"That's true," she said. "Which is why I wanted to talk to you alone. Grace and Havana are seniors. They graduate at the end of the spring and can do whatever they want. But you have a whole other year left, as I understand it, yes?"

"Yeah, it would take at least one really big semester or two small ones to get the credits I need."

"That's what I thought," she said. "These are papers that I had drafted by the school and the heads of your scholarship programs. As you know, one of the requirements of your scholarship was your continued play on one of our squads. But there is an exception. If you are picked for a national team, you can pause your studies and your scholarship with no penalty for up to four years."

"Oh wow," I said. I was getting dizzy and felt like I couldn't breathe in enough oxygen. This was everything I had ever hoped for with softball, and so many things I never thought I would achieve.

"Additionally," she said, "the school is willing to offer a supplemental scholarship on the basis of you returning to school either upon not making the Olympic team or after the Olympic competitions next summer. It would be at the same rate your scholarship pays now but without having to pay for books or classes, it would mean that money would be expected to help you travel and survive while you are playing and representing our school on the national squad.

"Now, the question is"—she finally let the smile run wild, stretching from ear to ear—"is this something you are interested in?"

"Of course it is!" I nearly shouted, feeling like I was vibrating in my seat. "I can't believe it."

"Well, believe it, kid. You've been incredible this season. I am very, very proud of you. And while I personally will miss having you on the team next year, if it means you are competing on the national team and Olympics, I am sure I will find a way."

"Thank you, Coach," I said, tears streaming down my cheeks without bothering to check with the brain if I thought that was okay. The emotion was taking over, and I was becoming a mess of smiling, giggling, crying, and sweating. Mostly sweating. I felt like my entire body was on fire.

"You are most welcome. But remember, you made this happen, not me. I simply put you in a position to succeed. You had to pull your weight, and you did and then some. You are every bit as capable of being on the Olympic team as any other girl I have ever seen play."

"Thank you," I choked out. "That really means so much, thank you."

"All right, enough of the mushy stuff. Come over here and give me a hug and head on out. Take these papers with you. They are consent forms and a form for your intention to return to school after your time on the national and/or Olympic team is finished."

I stood, trying to wipe tears out of my eyes and off my cheeks without making a big deal out of it and gave her a hug over the desk. She handed me the envelope, and I turned, opened the door, and shut it behind me as I walked through.

Then I squealed.

I could hardly believe it. I had worked so hard for this moment. So much practice, grinding through games, and yes, studying with Gavin to keep my grades up had gone into this. Now I was on the precipice of realizing my dreams.

There were a dozen people I wanted to share this with immediately. One, of course, was Gavin. I knew how proud he would be, how encouraging he would be like he always was. But I kind of wanted to save him for last. It would be all the sweeter if he were the last to know.

Then again, he was on campus. The news would filter to him rather quickly if I didn't get ahold of him fast. One of the other people I wanted to tell was one of the more likely ones to spill the news. Emma. I wanted to share it with her because we were so close, but also to make sure she didn't mention anything to Gavin. I wanted to tell him myself.

As I pulled open the phone to dial her, my thumb hovered over my mother's number. A part of me felt a responsibility to tell her first. But at the same time, she had never been supportive of me playing sports. Dad was always mildly supportive, in that way that he was supportive of anything I wanted to do, but Mom was usually against it. She would probably react like it was no big deal unless I told her I was on the Olympic team. Even then, she'd probably start every conversation about me with, "You know my daughter is an Olympian. I know, it's just *softball*, but you know, they have so many games now."

No, I didn't deserve to destroy my good feelings by letting her take the wind out of my sails. I was going to talk to people who would be just as excited for me as I was. Or close, at least.

Scrolling down, I found Emma's number and punched it, pulling the phone to my ear as I made my way into the lobby of the large gym. The phone rang twice before it picked up. There was a pause before anyone said anything and I almost said something before I was cut off.

"Hello?" Emma's voice came through.

"Emma! I just got out of the meeting with Coach Sam!"

"Oh my goodness, is it what I thought it was?"

"They want me on the national team, and I'm trying out for the Olympics in the fall!"

"It is!"

There was a squealing sound from both of us that went on for much longer than what I considered the non-embarrassing amount. When we both calmed, my voice was still echoing in the thankfully empty lobby.

"I am so happy for you, Lila. And so, so proud. You deserve this. You absolutely deserve this."

"Thank you, Emma," I said. "You know I couldn't have done it without my all-star catcher."

"Psh," she said. "Bitch, you are damn near an Olympian. I'm a decent backstop. Don't fluff me up. You deserve this entirely on your own."

"Oh man, I can't believe it," I said, sitting on one of the stone benches in the lobby and putting my head in my hand. My cheeks felt sore from smiling so hard. This had been one hell of a happy twenty-four hours.

"So when are you coming back over to Gavin's?" she asked.

"Why?" I asked. "Are you still there?"

"I am," she said in a sing-songy voice. "These boys are... not good at cleaning up after themselves. I'm being a bit of a domesticated woman for the moment."

"You?" I asked. "That's a departure from the norm."

"I know, right?" she laughed. "Something about this boy, Lila, I don't mind telling you. I want him to wife me, like, pronto."

"Wow," I said. "You were never the settle down type. What changed?"

"Babe, being with Kevin is *not* settling down. It's just having a partner to be wild with."

I laughed. Kevin's open-minded nature wasn't a secret, though he was usually immune to any picking on for it, being almost seven feet tall and able to crush apples in one hand. People thought twice about calling him names.

"Well, whatever floats your boat," I said.

"I have a dozen different innuendoes about boats, but I am going to refrain from using them because this call is about you," she said.

I laughed again.

"Thank you, Emma," I said. "And to answer your question, I have another class."

"Okay, that works," she said. "I'll make everyone lunch then."

"Sounds good, I'll be there in a couple hours. On another subject, you didn't talk to Gavin before he left, did you?"

"I did, but briefly," she said.

"You didn't tell him what was going on with me today, with the meeting with Coach or anything did you?"

"I might have," she said hesitantly. "I told him Coach was looking for you."

"Ahh," I said, a little disappointed. "Oh well, if you talk to him again, don't repeat what I told you. As a matter of fact, don't tell anyone. I want Gavin to hear it from me."

"Got it," she said. "See you in a bit. I have to clean this oven."

I laughed again. It was so weird to hear her on a cleaning spree. Not that she was a sloppy person, but I just had this image of a suddenly domesticated Emma, and it was just not fitting.

"All right, see you then."

I hung up and immediately tried Gavin's number. If he knew where I was, he'd probably put it together what it was about. I just didn't want him getting confirmation from anyone but me.

His phone didn't even ring. It went straight to voicemail.

That was weird.

I tried again, and again it went to voicemail.

He must have either turned it off while in class, which was a requirement of some of our professors, or he'd let it die and it was on a charger somewhere or waiting to be charged. Either way, I decided a text would get to him first when he got his phone back on, so I pulled up a chat window.

"I have some amazing news. Can we meet up before you go home?"

Chapter Sixteen

Gavin

"WHAT THE HELL ARE YOU doing here?"

"Gavin, please," Mom said, taking a step toward me. I didn't move. I wasn't going to run and embrace her, nor was I going to walk away. But I didn't have any patience for her bullshit, and I was fairly certain my stance gave that away.

"Please what?" I asked.

"Do you have a minute? Just a minute, to talk to me, your mother? Please?"

"I have class," I said.

"Please, Gavin, just a minute. It will be short, I promise. I just need to talk to you."

I looked at my phone to check the time and then let my head fall back as I clenched my eyes. I didn't need this shit today. Or ever, really. I would be happy never really seeing either of my parents again. But of the two, Mom was better. I could believe she was just terrible at the job of being a mother and clueless as to how to get better. At least she wasn't actively trying to be worse, like Dad always was.

Not that Mom was good. Just not as bad.

"All right," I sighed. "One minute. I don't want to be late."

"One minute," she said. "If I can fit it all, yes. Thank you."

"Come over here," I said, beckoning her to a bench by the building I needed to go in. If it got bad, I could always just nope out of there and go in the building. If I shut it behind me, she wouldn't be able to get in without a key or by slipping in behind another student, which would technically be trespassing.

We sat down on the bench, and I turned so I could face her, one leg lying sideways. The leg that still had a massive bruise down the thigh. It wasn't lost on me that the pain I was feeling was indirectly her fault.

"Okay," I said. "Go."

She took a deep breath, letting it out slowly and shaking a little like she was holding back tears. I should have felt some empathy for her in that moment, but I just couldn't. She had faked tears so often in the past that I didn't feel like I needed to get myself worked up until I saw some action behind them.

"All right," she said. "First, I want to thank you. I know you gave up your scholarship to save me, and that was something that you didn't have to do, and I didn't want you to do. Not after I got to thinking about it. My past and present shouldn't ruin your future. But you did it, and it saved my life, and I want to thank you for that."

I nodded. I didn't want to tell her she was welcome because, frankly, she wasn't. I resented every bit of it. But I wasn't just saving her ass with that payment. I was saving my own. They could have broken my arm to bits, and I would never pitch again. I was lucky that it was just sore from being reset and needed time to get better.

"Okay," I choked out, for lack of better anything else.

"I need you to know I won't be in contact for a few months," she said. Immediately I thought she was running away or hiding from someone else now and was going to ask me for money. I steeled myself to tell her no. "I am going to rehab."

"Oh," I said, suddenly taken aback. Never, in my entire life, had my mother ever admitted she had a problem. She'd yelled at Dad for *his* but had never admitted her own alcohol and drug issues. It felt revelatory. "I think that is a very good choice for you."

"Me too," she said. "I found a place out in Arizona. Lots of sun, living in these little huts. There's a pool and a golf course and a tennis court. I can get out and do stuff or just sit in the desert and commune with nature. But no drugs. No alcohol. Not even soda is allowed. No meat, either, which might be a challenge. All vegetarian, and only water. No sugar either."

"Wow," I said. "How long?"

"Eight weeks," she said. "Then I am going to head to Salt Lake. Do you remember your aunt Patsy?"

"No," I said. "I don't. Sorry."

"It's okay," she said. "She only saw you a few times when you were little. She was my mother's sister, but they were estranged for years. She had moved to Utah and settled down out there with her partner. They run a theater."

"Cool," I said.

"It is cool," she said. "She said I could move out there and live with her for a while and work in the theater. Doing some cleaning, ticket taking, that sort of thing. She said she'd teach me how to do makeup and I could make some money until I could get a place of my own. I think I might stay out there, though. Patsy is straight-edge. Apparently, that means no drugs or alcohol?"

"It does," I said. "It's a movement among a lot of younger people."

"Well, she has it tattooed down her arms," she laughed. "She's a funny old lady. Tough as nails. Her lifestyle is so... different."

"I bet," I said. "So you're going to be gone for a while then?"

"Yes," she said, turning her watery red eyes to me. "For a long time, I think. But at least for a few months. You never know how you will gel with people until you live with them, and everything could fall apart out there, but I'm going to try. I'm going to try really hard. Because this is my one shot."

I nodded. There was a looming question in the air, but it felt like neither one of us wanted to say anything about it. I cleared my throat trying to find the words when she took a breath in and let it out slowly again.

"I'm splitting up with your father, too," she said. "He's not a big fan of the idea, but we have no property, you're an adult and I don't want, nor could I get alimony. So I'm divorcing him."

"Honestly, I think that's for the best," I said.

"Me too," she said. "I wish I had done it a long time ago. I was just too scared, too caught up in the life I was living. I am only sorry I made you live in that world with us."

I nodded. "It wasn't great."

"But you got out," she said. "And you've made something of yourself. And you are going to continue to make something of yourself. I believe that. You're going to be an amazing person for the rest of your life. If I did nothing else of any worth on this planet my whole life, at least I brought you into it."

I didn't know how to respond to that, so I just looked down at my shoes and kicked a piece of gravel.

"Your father, by the way," she continued, "will be in prison for at least five years. That's the first time he will be eligible for parole. I'm not sure if he will get it with all his priors, but he might. So just keep an eye on that."

"What about you?" I asked. "Do you think he will come after you?"

"Not if I'm near Aunt Patsy," she laughed. "That woman scares the shit out of him."

I laughed.

"Well, good," I said. "That all sounds good. How long is his sentence for?"

"Ten," she said. "But he doesn't have any weapons charges or anything. Just the fights he got popped for and the possession charges. So my guess is he's out in five to seven."

I nodded.

"The biker gang leaving you alone?" I asked.

"Yes," she said. "Thank you. Those men are awful, but they finally just stopped coming around. I moved out of the house and into a tiny apartment. I was thinking about renting it out, but I've got a guy that wants to buy it. He's a slumlord, and he's offering me like two-thirds of what it's worth, but I'm going to take it anyway. It's just bad memories there. And I can use the money to pay for rehab and to start over."

"Doesn't Dad get some of that?" I asked.

"House is in my name." She smiled. "He made me put it in my name. I can sell it and do what I want with the money until the divorce is finalized. By then, I won't have much of it left. He's free to sue me for it."

"Good," I said. "He doesn't deserve shit."

"No, he doesn't," she said. "It does lead me to another question, though. I have all your stuff in storage. I moved it there after the last time you came over. I just didn't trust your father not to go in there and try to find stuff he could sell. You know how he was."

"Yeah, I do," I said bitterly. The memories of various nice things I had in the past that 'went missing' right before Dad suddenly came home with a new TV or was gone for a week on some bender were at the forefront of my mind.

"It's at the place right at the corner, you know, where your dad practiced in that awful band that never did a show when you were a teen?"

"I remember," I said. "If you can just send me a copy of the key and the lot number, I'll go get my stuff in the next couple weeks."

"You're free to anything in there," she said. "Anything you don't want to take, I'm going to tell them they can have and sell off. I don't want any of it. Everything that was mine went with me to the hotel."

"Okay," I said. "Is the old couch in there?"

The look on her face was worth the silly question.

"Oh, heck not, Gavin, you don't want that thing. I only put it in storage because I forgot to have them drop it off at the dump and it was easier that way."

"I was kidding," I said. "I don't want it. It was a joke."

"Oh, thank goodness," she said, shaking her head.

The couch in question was at least thirty years old, probably more. It had at one time been white, with purple and pink streaks in random places. The encapsulation of shopping mall '90s aesthetics. It had been a purchase Dad had made when he moved out on his own as a teen and had been with him ever since, even at the argument of my mother. She wanted to set it on fire.

Years of drunken escapades, various moves, then a child's penchant for spilling the milk in their cereal bowl later and it was a lumpy, smelly, barely still stitched-together mess. The cushions held almost no support, and you could feel the springs under your ass in most of it. It was the worst couch I could imagine still being in regular use, mostly when Dad came home drunk or high and passed out on it.

"I'm glad you came to talk to me," I said, surprising even myself. "I mean, I'm glad to hear all this. I hoped, for a long time, that you would figure a way out of this mess. I hope you know I just can't deal with any of it right now. It's too much. I gave up a lot to save you guys, and now I have to focus on me."

"Of course," she said. "I get it. Honestly, you are a saint for dealing with it all the way up to now. I ... I know I haven't been a good mother to you. And I am so, so sorry for that. But I am going to try to be better from now on."

"Thank you," I said.

"Can I have a hug?"

"Yeah," I said, for the first time in a long, long time not resisting.

She wrapped her arms around me, and for just a split second, I was a kid again. A kid who didn't understand his parents' problems but loved them anyway with the innocence of a child. I closed my eyes and hugged her tight, just like I did then, hoping that that love might be enough to fix them.

"I'm proud of you, Mom," I said. "Let me know when you get to the rehab place and then let me know when you're heading to Utah, okay?"

"I will," she said. "And I'll send you that key to the storage soon. If you have the key to the house still, it's mostly empty, but anything left in there is free to you as well."

"Thanks, Mom."

"I love you, son," she said, clearly holding back tears.

"I love you too, Mom."

With that, she hugged me tight again and then walked away. I watched her go for a few minutes, wondering if this was for real or just another chapter in the long book of her screw-ups. I decided I was going to at least hope for it being real.

My phone vibrated in my pocket, and I realized I had put it on silent. It had been going off for a bit. I pulled it out and checked my texts. There was one from Lila, but my phone was almost dead. The screen was so dark I couldn't read it. I shoved it back in my pocket and headed into class, which had already started, figuring I could charge it inside while class went on.

Chapter Seventeen

Lila

I NEEDED TO STOP BY my place before I met with Gavin, just in case. Even the idea of that excited me and added to the general elation of the day. I might get to top all this off by roaming my hands over his muscled core while he used his magic tongue to bring me to ecstasy. I'd say that would be the capper on just about the best day I had ever had.

The only issue, of course, was going back to my apartment and getting stuff out, and in doing so, dealing with Star. I was still weirded out by how she'd acted earlier and didn't know what to think about it. I didn't feel *unsafe*, per se. But I did feel strange about how she was acting.

But that was silly, wasn't it? She had explained her side well enough, albeit as if it were barely a thought. She was an artist and known for being wild and weird and acting strange for no particular reason. I just needed to let it go on my side, and I would probably see her behavior as nothing more than normal 'Weird Star Shit.'

Heading back to the apartment, I made a list of what I needed to pack in my phone. I wanted to be able to stay there as long as I felt welcome. Selfishly, I hoped it would be more than a day, but I was going to play it by ear. If I felt like it might be good to have some space, only to keep from wearing out my welcome, I would go home.

I wondered if Star would have any idea how important what had just happened to me was. She had listened to me talk about softball before, but I got the impression that none of it had stuck. It just wasn't of interest to her, so it didn't stay around in her brain. But she had always seemed happy for me when I was happy, and when she had her more lucid moments, like around Thanksgiving, she could come down to Earth a bit and engage.

Not that I expected her to after the display this morning.

When I opened the door, however, it had somehow been even worse than I expected.

Food and dishes and art supplies were everywhere. Teetering on top of stacks of crumpled papers was a plate with leftover spaghetti on it. A cereal bowl was in the center of the living room table. It looked uneaten. It looked like every glass or cup we owned was around the room, with various amounts of water in them. It was like a bomb had gone off.

It made me angry, honestly. Star never kept up after herself, but she had barely been here alone for any length of time, and she caused this? And clearly, she simply expected me to clean it. It had been an agreement we entered early on that I regretted. I would keep the place up, and she would pay for the electricity and the streaming network payments. They would come automatically off the card her father gave her.

Usually, I was able to intervene before the major messes happened, keeping up with her as she laid down dishes and clothes and whatever else she suddenly decided she didn't want to be holding but had a mental block as to what to do with it. This time, however, I hadn't been there, and the explosion was intense.

Sighing, I grabbed a TV tray that we had in the kitchen, usually used to hold bananas and apples, and filled it with glasses. I had just brought them into the kitchen, opened up the dishwasher, and began putting them in when Star came out of her room and stood in the doorway.

"Hey," she began.

"What the hell, Star?" I asked.

"I'm sorry?"

"I leave for like five seconds, and I come back to this? It's a freaking wreck. Dishes everywhere, clothes all over the place, food everywhere. Hell, I hope you didn't eat any of that after it sat out for a while. Did you empty the dehumidifier? Because it's full right now. Have you emptied it at all?"

"N-no," she said, her wide, blue, doe eyes looking like they might tear up.

No. I can't be swayed by her baby deer impression.

"This is ridiculous," I said. "You are an adult, Star. I've had one of the best pieces of news ever, and all I wanted was to come home and tell you and grab some stuff so I could go somewhere else tonight, and I walk in on the place looking like this."

"I'm... I'm sorry," Star said. "You've never yelled at me before."

"I haven't?" I asked. It was more like thundered, but the problem was, all the venom was gone. Her expression was so earnest, so pure, that it was hard to keep being mad at her. It was like she had no idea the place had gotten bad.

"No," she said, her eyes still wide and brimming with tears as she shook her head. Blond locks fell in front of her face and pushed a droplet down her cheek. The effect was like I had kicked a puppy.

It was the first time I had ever seen Star be affected like this. She normally never really showed any emotion. Curiosity and mild amusement were just about all I ever got, except when she would suddenly become the girl who wanted to talk about boys, and then it would go away a day later and she'd be back to this.

It was unnerving.

"Look," I said, "I'm sorry for snapping at you, okay? I just get really frustrated when you do this. I know I usually keep up the place, but to make this big of a mess in that short of a time, it just seems like you did it on purpose."

"I didn't," she said. "I've... I've just had a very bad couple of days, okay? It's been really difficult."

Shit. Here it came. The waterworks were because I stole her boyfriend. I knew she wasn't okay with all that.

I was the bad guy.

"Star," I began, trying to form the world's worst apology in my mind. An apology that would end with "but I am still going to date him, because there's no way in hell I would let him go."

"It's just the people I was with in France—" she began. I rolled my eyes. So it wasn't me or Gavin. It was more humblebragging. Only minus some of the humbleness. I guess that's just called bragging, isn't it?

"Ah," I said.

"They were great, really," she said. "We had a ton of fun, and I saw all those cool things, and I got to do painting in the fields and see all these museums. It's just... it's just like, I got home, and none of it *mattered*. You know? It was just time that I spent. I was happy to have done those things, and I can always look back on them and say, yes, I did that, but what did I get out of it? Nothing. I got nothing out of it.

"Painting in France was like painting here. Doing sculpture in France was like doing sculpture in my bedroom. Nothing was different but the scenery. And it was beautiful, don't get me wrong, but I just... I didn't care. It was just scenery. I spent all that time away, all that money, and I feel like I let you down, all to do nothing. Nothing of consequence anyway."

"Oh," I said. This had to be the most Star had spoken in one continuous moment in the entire time I'd known her. And she wasn't done. I leaned against the sink and crossed my arms. All the anger was gone now.

"I realized something while I was there. Maybe that realization is the reason I needed to go, but it feels hollow. I realized that I don't need to be anywhere else. I am at my happiest, my most creative, when I am here, at this apartment. With you. And sometimes with Gavin. This is my safe space.

"And what's more, I don't even know if it has anything to do with this apartment. I think my safe space is just being around you. You are so different from me, Lila. But you're real. I don't even feel like I'm real, you know? I just... exist. I create. But I don't live. And I don't even want to. I just want to create. I want to produce art that makes people feel something."

"Okay," I said, more or less just to show I was still paying attention. Her eyes were still watery, but they were focused. On me. She wasn't just talking to the room at large, like she seemed to always do. She was speaking right to me. I felt exposed in a way. This was all very, very dramatic, but unlike other dramatic things with Star, it felt incredibly authentic.

"I create. It's how I communicate with the rest of the world. It's how I show emotion. It's how I talk. It's the lens that I see the world through. It's a window, both for things to go in and come out of. I know I've been babied for a long time. My parents babied me, then you did. You took care of me, kept the house up, made sure I remembered to pay bills. I exist as a functional adult in this world only because you come up after me and make sure I do. I thank you for it. And I apologize for it. I hate that I am a burden to you, ever. I feel so bad about it. But, Lila, I don't want you to go anywhere. I don't want you to leave me alone. I don't think I can handle it."

I was dumbfounded.

This was, by far, the most Star had ever opened up. Sure, she had told me all kinds of things about art or her family, but there was always a separation there. Like she was just rattling off facts she knew. This was real. This was her soul. She was telling me as best she could how she felt. And I heard her.

She didn't want me to go, and now that I was with Gavin, she was afraid I would. Hell, I was already spending nights over at his place. I got it. She was like a child in a lot of ways, afraid of the dark and of being alone. I could understand that.

I opened my arms and walked toward her. Star nearly fell apart in tears, but she crossed the space between us at a run and wrapped her arms around my shoulders. I held her tight, rubbing her back.

"I'm not going anywhere," I said. "Don't worry about that. You are my best friend. I won't just leave you, okay?"

She nodded, tears staining my shirt.

"But I need you to know something, okay?" I asked, pulling her to arm's length. "Gavin and I are dating. And it might be pretty serious already. I will most likely be spending a lot of time with him. But I am not abandoning you."

She nodded again. "I understand," she said. "I just don't want to be like my mother. Alone. On some island. Painting the same painting of the ocean over and over because she pushed everyone else away being a self-centered artist. She is so terribly alone. I can't be like her. I can't survive like that."

"You won't have to," I said. "We may not live together forever, but I'm not going anywhere just yet, okay?"

"All right," she said, a small smile pulling at one side of her mouth.

"Look," I said, in a moment of empathy, "why don't you come over to Gavin's for dinner? I know Emma is planning on making lunch, but I can push that an hour or so later, and we can all do dinner. How's that sound?"

"That sounds amazing," she said. "Thank you, Lila."

"You're welcome, Star," I said, hugging her again. "Now, can you take care of these dishes? And clothes?"

"Yes," she said. "I'll do it right now. I'll meet you guys there. Just tell me when. I have something I need to finish in my room."

"Good, I will. I have a text to send and some stuff to grab."

Smiling and wondering what I'd just done, I walked into the bedroom and shut the door. Clearly, I felt bad for her, in a way I had never thought to feel for her before. She was a mess. But she was *my* mess. As her friend, it was my duty to help her.

I pulled out my phone and pulled up the message thread with Emma. She had texted me a few minutes before, and I hadn't seen it yet. She was asking if I would rather do dinner instead. I grinned.

"That sounds amazing," I said. "Can we handle one more?"

"Sure," she texted back almost instantly. "Who?"

"Star," I texted. She responded with a shocked emoji. Funnily enough, that was my own response too.

Chapter Eighteen

Gavin

I KEPT GLANCING OVER at the phone the entire time class was going. My charger was acting up, and if it slipped just the slightest bit, it would stop charging. When it did, I would have to gently nudge it back into place, while continuing to pay attention to the professor.

Professor Martin was one of those older professors who had no patience for smartphones. If he saw you fiddling with one during a class, he would send you out. I'd happened to be lucky enough to slide into class and find a spot right by a wall outlet, and when the lights were dimmed, I plugged the charger in. It had gone completely dead, and while it charged, I just wanted to turn it on and respond to Lila.

Finally, when the class was over, I yanked the charger out of the wall, determined to go get a new one later, and turned on the phone. Thirty-five percent was going to have to do. I swept up to open the message thread with Lila.

She had sent a couple new ones since the one I got, all about meeting up later. Now, apparently, we were going to meet at my place for dinner, which Emma was cooking. I knew absolutely nothing about how well Emma cooked. It made me want to stuff a burger in my face first, just in case. If anyone might know if she was decent, it would be Lila, so I went ahead and punched the button to call her.

"Hey you," she said.

"Hey. So. What's this about dinner with Emma tonight?"

"She offered," she said. "She wanted to make dinner and be domestic. I think she's just trying to impress Kevin, but she wants us all there tonight."

"What time?" I asked.

"About an hour or so."

"Ahh, well, see, I'm starving," I said. "Do we know how good a cook Emma is? Should I grab a burger or something beforehand?"

"Well, to be honest, I don't know. I've never seen her cook. But her dad is a chef, so I would hope she knows a few things."

"Hmmm. Do you want a burger?"

"Probably?" she said. "I mean, maybe grab a couple and then bring them over and keep them in your room. That way if Emma can't cook, we can retire to your room and eat."

"That sounds like a plan," I said. "All right, I'll see you there."

"Wait," she said. "There's something else."

"Oh? What's up?"

"Star is coming."

I froze where I was, mid-stride, and took a seat on a nearby bench.

"Star is what?"

"She's going to be there," Lila said. "She's coming to dinner."

"What? Why?"

"I think... I think everything is okay with us now. All three of us. I'm pretty sure of it," she said. "Like ninety percent sure."

"What's the other ten percent?" I asked.

"She might also murder us all."

"Well, that's certainly not a risk I like taking," I said.

"She's weird. I mean, she's always weird, but she's been weird even for Star. Whatever is going to happen, I would assume we'd know by the end of dinner though. So, yay?"

"Yay," I said, with no emotion. "Are you sure you think this is a good idea?"

"I think it's the best idea I have at the moment. You and Kevin are big guys. If she whips out a knife, I'm sure one of you could take her."

"I'm sure of that," I said.

"But if she's been making some kind of art-bomb-project, we have a whole other problem," she interrupted.

"Ah. Yes. That would be bad."

"Anyway, I'll see you in about an hour. I like pickles on my burgers. No mayo."

"Got it," I said. "See you then."

I hung up not knowing exactly how to feel about all this. It was going to be a weird evening, for sure, but if it meant putting everything behind us and me being able to move forward with Lila, I was for it. I headed toward home with a slight bit of optimism and a whole lot of worry.

I was a few blocks away when my phone rang. I pulled it out and was surprised to see Coach's name on the caller ID. Figuring I was going to be asked to watch some tape of the weekend's performance, I reluctantly answered.

"Hello?"

"Hey, Gavin. Can you come by the office for a few minutes? I need to speak with you. In person."

"Sure, what's up?"

"I just want to talk to you in person is all. When can you get down here?"

"I'm passing the gym now. I can be there in about five minutes."

"Perfect," he said. "I'll see you then, bud."

"Okay."

Coach hung up, and I shoved the phone in my pocket. That was weird. For one, Coach never called me 'bud.' For another, I couldn't remember the last time he was so vague about why he wanted to see me. He wasn't a guy that kept things under a lid very well. If he was mad about something, he tended to let you know. Loudly. Immediately.

I made my way to Coach's office, hoping it wouldn't take very long. I still needed to grab the burgers before I headed home. Plus, I was emotionally pretty drained already and wanted a little bit of time to decompress in my room. Encountering Mom and having that talk with her had taken a lot out of me.

Coach's door was shut, so I rapped on it with my knuckles. Coach said something that sounded like 'come in' in a muffled voice, and I opened the door.

He wasn't alone. A tall, serious-looking man with black-rimmed glasses was standing beside him. He was wearing a suit, and I could see a badge hanging from his neck. He didn't smile. Neither did Coach.

"Gavin, come on in, please. Shut the door behind you."

I did as I was asked and stepped into the room a bit farther.

"What's going on?" I asked.

"Gavin, this is Detective Eudy from Myrtle Beach. He would like to speak with you for a few minutes with me. Can you take a seat?"

"Sure," I said, my heart thumping in my chest. This did not look good.

Coach took off his reading glasses and squeezed the bridge of his nose for a moment, his eyes clamping shut. When he opened them again, he sat back in the chair and folded his hands over each other on his chest.

"Gavin, the detectives in Myrtle Beach have some really disturbing video of you. From the hotel cameras. Footage that I've seen. Footage that, quite frankly, could jeopardize your scholarship and even your entire career. And we need to know, right now, what your side of the story is."

My heart sank into my stomach. The rest of my life was going to go up in flames.

"Okay," I said. "I'll tell you anything you need to know."

"For what it's worth, Detective, I believe he will," Coach said.

"I'll judge that," the detective said. "Gavin Freeman, that is your name, correct?"

"Yes," I said.

"Son of Albert Freeman, currently serving time in the Georgia State Penitentiary?"

I sighed. "Yes."

"And you know why he is in prison?"

"Sort of," I said. "I tried to keep my life and his as separate as I could once I moved out."

The detective smirked, and I instantly disliked him. He was one of those people who thought the worst of everyone. You could feel it coming off him. I was sure he saw all kinds of terrible people in his line of work, but to judge people before you know anything about them takes a special type of douchebaggery.

"You did, huh?" he asked, sarcasm dripping off the words. "See, the problem I have with that is on this footage we have, we can see you clearly making a payment to a drug dealing biker. One that your father was in league with and may have taken the fall for with his prison term. And we have footage from the bank where you withdrew that money, and, well, it was a very large sum, Gavin."

"Yup," I said, wanting to get right to the heart of the matter. "You sure do."

"Gavin," Coach said in disbelief. I held up my hand.

"All the things you said are correct," I continued. "But you don't know the context. And you're missing a lot of information."

"Oh, I am?" Detective Eudy said. He was now sitting on the corner of Coach's desk, crowding my personal space. It was a trick detectives did a lot, and I wasn't intimidated. I'd seen enough true crime shows and interviews with suspects to know the game. It was something Lila and I both enjoyed.

"Yes," I said. "Critical shit that I am surprised you didn't bring up. Unless you just thought you were going to drop a hammer on me and catch me in a lie, I suppose?"

"Please, do tell me what evidence I have. I'd love to hear that," he said, smirking and crossing his arms over his chest. Coach was now leaning forward, his fingers interlaced and pressing his lips against them, almost like he was praying.

"Well, for one, if you bothered to look at the tape from a day before, you'd see those same gang members in a fight with me and Kevin. A hellacious street fight in the parking lot. One where I beat their asses, but they nearly broke my arm. And since I'm not a gang fighter and they are, they were able to coerce me into giving them that money with threats to me, my friends and my family."

The detective brightened up a little. He took a moment to look up at the ceiling before looking back down at Coach, then me.

"You were right, Coach. He's rather honest."

"Excuse me? What the hell is going on? You got into a *street fight* before a tournament where scouts would be watching? What the hell is wrong with you?" Coach thundered.

"I didn't start it," I said. "I was followed and attacked. I only defended myself."

"But... why? And why didn't you tell someone? We could have contacted authorities, gotten them involved," he continued.

"Because they would have killed my mother," I interrupted. The room went deathly silent.

"What?" Coach asked.

"My father is in prison, but frankly, that was a godsend. In prison, he has at least some modicum of protection. Out in the wild, well, he owed the bikers all that money. Every cent of what I gave them, all my scholarship money, all that was to pay off his debt. I didn't have a choice."

"What happened exactly?" Detective Eudy asked. "Start from the beginning."

Twenty minutes later, I had recounted the entire story back to Detective Eudy and Coach. Coach was in a state of near tears. He'd clearly had no idea and was blindsided by all this.

"So have you heard from your mother since then?" Detective Eudy asked.

"I heard from her today, actually. She came to campus to tell me she is leaving for rehab. I won't have contact with her again for a few months at the earliest."

"Dammit," he said. "All right, well, she's out as a witness unless we can track her down. But I need to know if you would be willing to testify to what you told me today."

"Yes."

It was without hesitation. I wasn't afraid anymore.

"You will testify in a courtroom to what you just said?" he asked again.

"Yes."

"All right," he said, standing up and grabbing his jacket off the coat rack in the corner of the room. "Coach, I know this is your office, but I need to ask you a favor."

"Favor?" Coach asked, clearly in his own world of spinning thoughts and panic. His job security depended on the team, and me being on the team was a big part of it.

"Yes," Eudy said. "Could we have the room, please? Like I said, I know this is your office, but I would like to speak to Gavin privately."

"Sure," Coach said.

"Also," Eudy said, stopping him before he could pass, "don't make any plans about Gavin other than what you would normally do. For right now, nothing has changed. I'm not charging him with anything yet. I may not at all. But I need cooperation from everyone involved not to tip anyone off and to remain as normal. Is that understood?"

"Yes," Coach said, his eyes so wide I thought they might fall out of his head. "I understand."

"All right then," Eudy said. "I appreciate your help in this matter, Coach. I will let you know by text when we are done in here, and you may resume whatever it was you were doing."

"Just... doing tape research," he mumbled, almost to himself, as he turned to leave. "See you later, Gavin."

"Bye, Coach," I said, as he stumbled through the door. When it shut behind him, I looked up at Eudy.

"He'll be fine," Eudy said. "Now let's go over a few more things."

Chapter Nineteen

Lila

WHEN I GOT TO GAVIN'S apartment, I knew he wouldn't be home yet and figured I would be spending some quality time with Kevin and Emma. It wasn't exactly high on my list of encounters at the moment, mostly because of how awkwardly fast both of our relationships had developed, and I didn't want to be asked a bunch of questions nor hear a bunch of details that I was sure Emma was brimming with. That said, I was still surprised when the door opened, and Emma was on the other side.

"Hey," I said.

"Hey, come on in," she said. "I'm just about to put the pasta on."

"Pasta?" I asked.

"Yeah, well, see, I have a recipe for a really good sauce, but that's about the extent of my cooking skills," she said, darting off to the living room, where she picked up a rag and a spray bottle and began franticly wiping the coffee table down. "I just figured if I have one shot to make a first impression, I should do what I know, then teach myself everything else as I go."

"Sure," I said, taking off my purse and hanging it from the coat rack. "I just thought dinner wasn't for a few more hours."

"Oh, it isn't," she said. "I just like to have the pasta cooked and out of the way early. Little bit of butter keeps them from sticking together and getting hard and then I plop them in the sauce at the last minute to warm up."

"Oh," I said. "Smart."

She stood up suddenly, beaming. "Thanks," she said.

"So what's all this then?"

I gestured to the various cleaning supplies lying around. This included a hamper of what I assumed were Kevin's clothes by the length of the massive pair of jeans.

"I, uh... I've been doing some cleaning while Kevin was in class."

"I can see that, but why?"

Her cheeks reddened as she pulled a strand of hair away from her face, then headed to the kitchen to stir the sauce again.

"I just... I don't know," she said. "I think, and I know this is crazy, so don't start any shit about it, but... I think I'm in ... *love*?"

"Whoa," I said.

"I know, right?" she said. "I just don't have any other words that seem to describe it, and I don't know that there are any, to be honest. I've just gotten all stupid over Kevin."

"I can see that," I said. "I never pegged you for the domesticated type."

"I'm not!" she said. "I mean, I never have been, at least. I'm generally pretty tidy, but I tend to not pick up after other people. But something about Kevin, I just want to take care of him, you know? I want to know he has a nice, clean place and all his things are taken care of. So when he sees his empty laundry basket, he will think of me, and how I did that for him, and oh my goodness I sound like an idiot."

I laughed. "I mean, you aren't winning feminist of the year with any of this your saying," I said.

She hung her head. "I am a strong woman who don't need no man," she grumbled sadly at the pot as she stirred again.

"Clearly."

"Lila, I don't know. I just really like him. And I feel like I want to take care of him. Am I crazy?"

"No," I said, sighing and joining her in the kitchen. "Need help with anything?"

"Other than my broken brain, no," she said. "I could use a glass of wine if you could pour me one, though."

"That I can do," I said. I took a look at the various bottles sitting on the bottom shelf of the refrigerator and tapped my chin. "Umm, do you know anything about wine?"

"Other than it was the only alcohol my parents let me have because they gave it to me at mass? No. Not really."

"Well, there are a bunch of bottles in here, and I know wine can be expensive. I think rosé is good for just drinking?"

"Sure?" she said. "I'll replace it if it's something he was keeping. I just feel like I could use a glass of something with alcohol in it to calm my nerves, and I don't think they keep whiskey around here."

I brought the bottle out of the fridge and grabbed a wine glass out of a cabinet and sat them down on the counter. Then I went about the search for a wine cork.

"Any ideas on a corkscrew?" I asked.

"None at all," she said. "I'm not entirely sure Kevin doesn't just use The Force to get them out. I wouldn't put it past him."

"Like *Star Wars*?" I asked, not shocked, but taken aback a bit that Emma would ever use a reference from a series that I considered a nerdy guilty pleasure.

"You know," she said, then held out an open hand with the fingers just barely clenched and made a whirring sound with her mouth. "The Force."

"I know what The Force is," I said. "I'm just surprised *you* know what The Force is."

"My dad and I used to watch them all the time when I was little," she said. "Kevin has the whole series on DVD in his room. We actually watched one while we fell asleep last night. Or, well, at least it was on in the background."

"Ah," I said, hoping that would be the end of it.

"Just as a heads-up, if a box shows up here with a slave Leia costume, that's for me. I might have ordered it this morning."

No such luck, I guessed. At least I found the wine screw. I opened the bottle and poured out a glass, handing it to Emma.

"So this thing is serious," I said, hoping to change the subject, and if not, at least direct it a little in another direction.

"Yes," she said, her shoulders slumping and a stupefied grin on her face. "He's just... I don't know, Lila. I've known him for so long, but we didn't really talk. You know? And now we just found so much we have in common, and so many things we don't that are just so *interesting*. I feel like every day is some big adventure of what am I going to find out about him now."

"That I understand," I said. "I feel the same way about Gavin."

"Yeah!" she exclaimed, suddenly turning on me so fast she flung red sauce on the cabinet. "About that! How have we not talked about you and Gavin yet?!"

"Because it's kind of just brand new!" I said. "Like, really, really new. Like yesterday officially new."

She squealed and did what I could only assume was an interpretive dance.

"Okay, so if it started yesterday, *officially*, then what was all that at the hotel?"

"Nothing," I said. "I mean, not nothing, but nothing relationship-wise. We might have kissed on the beach though..."

"YOU KISSED ON THE BEACH?!"

It was so loud, I was fairly certain all of Gavin's neighbors were now aware of where our first kiss had been.

"Yes," I said, my eyes wide and in a calm voice. "But I broke everything off because he was still technically with Star, and I didn't want to... do... anything. Oh shit. I invited Star. She's coming. She's coming here tonight, and I invited her and I just realized that maybe that was a stupid thing to do."

"Inviting your boyfriend's ex-girlfriend over for dinner when your relationship is less than thirty-six hours old? Yeah, that might not have been the best plan, girly."

"Shit. Shit, shit, shit."

"It'll be fine," Emma said, seeming to have calmed a bit, though she was still stirring the sauce so excitedly I wasn't sure any heat was actually touching it. "I'm sure Star will be an adult about it all; otherwise she wouldn't have said yes."

"Maybe," I said. My mind was working in overdrive. Maybe the reason Gavin didn't answer his phone was because I'd invited Star to dinner. Maybe he was having second thoughts. Maybe he was going to come to dinner tonight and tell me that he made a terrible mistake and he and Star would kick me out and I would be alone at the apartment knowing they were banging boots in his bedroom.

I shuddered.

"Seriously, it'll be fine," Emma said. "Besides, Kevin says that Star wasn't exactly his type anyway. Too spacey. He said he's never seen him as happy as he is when he's hanging out with you."

"Really?" I asked.

She nodded, taking a long sip of the wine.

"Yup," she said. "Also, excellent choice on this. Very yummy. Want some?"

"Sure," I said, defeated. I would rather stay stone cold sober, but now I was giving myself anxiety, and the thought of taking the edge off was very appealing. "Hand it over."

She filled a glass for me, and I took it, downing a good portion of it in one gulp. Emma shook her head.

"It's not beer, Lila," she said. "You're supposed to sip wine."

"Alcohol is alcohol," I said. "Fill 'er up again, please."

She topped me off, and I sat back on a chair in the dining room, turning it so I could face her.

"Well, at least were both going all silly over these boys together. It's kind of nice having someone I can squeal with."

"It is," I said, finding myself not lying about that either. "Good for us."

"Good for us," she repeated, picking up her glass and crossing over to me. She tinged it off mine and we both took probably-too-large sips.

I set the glass down and picked up my phone. Calling Gavin again, the call went right to voicemail. I didn't leave a message, instead stuffing the phone back into my pocket. One more thing to worry about, I guessed. Something else I was just going to have to wait and see about.

"Everything okay?" Emma asked, and I realized I had been sitting and staring into space for a few moments.

"Yeah," I said. "I guess."

"What's up?"

"I just... I worry about what Gavin is going to say about this national team offer," I said.

"You haven't told him yet?"

"I couldn't get ahold of him face to face," I said. "He had class, and then he said he was going to go do some errand and then come here. I wanted to tell him in person."

"That makes sense. It's super exciting," she said.

"It is," I said. "But I mean, we just got together. We haven't even really discussed what we are yet. And now I might be going to Florida to try out for the National Team and then traveling with them all over the world. And after that is the Olympic tryouts, and if I make that, then I'll be busy with that until next summer. That's a lot of me being gone."

"It is," she said. "But I am sure he will be happy for you. If what you have is strong enough, then you'll figure out how to make it work with all that distance."

"Yeah, but it isn't strong yet, right? It's a day old. Not even."

"It doesn't matter how *long* you've been together," Emma said. "It's how much you want to stay that way. Besides, you two have essentially been dating each other since last semester. You just called it hanging out with a friend."

I shrugged.

"Maybe," I said. "But Gavin is, well, *Gavin Freeman*. He's the star baseball player on campus. He could have any girl he wanted. Why would he want to wait on me to get back when he could literally have anyone?"

Emma put down the spatula and turned to face me. She had an expression that almost passed for anger, and she stomped over to me.

"I have half a mind to slap some sense into you, Lila," she said. "You are my friend, and I don't ever want to hear you talk about yourself like that again."

"What?"

"You are beautiful. Smart. Talented. Anyone would be lucky to have you in their life and interested in them. Anyone. Gavin might be famous and all on campus, but even he is smart enough to know when a real, genuine knockout, in every way imaginable, is not only an option, but super into him. If dating him is what you want to do, it doesn't matter what kind of schedule you have. He will figure it out. Or he's the dumbest man alive."

I didn't have words to respond to that. Instead, I simply stood and wrapped my friend in a hug. She squeezed me back, her head buried in my chest.

"Thank you," I said.

"No problem," she said. "Now I have to let you go because I'm going to suffocate in your giant knockers. Not that it's the worst way to go or anything, but I have shit to do."

I laughed. As worried as I was about tonight, and the future beyond it, at least I had one good friend I could depend on.

Unlike how I worried how Star would react.

Chapter Twenty

Gavin

"GAVIN, I HAVE A VERY serious question to ask you before you go," Eudy said.

"You mean I'm going to get to leave? Because I have a dinner to get to and some stuff I need to do before that."

He laughed. "Yes, you can leave, but first, I wanted to talk to you about something."

"Sure," I said, feeling relieved. A part of me thought I was going to be held in this office for a long time, until Eudy got some kind of confession out of me or something.

"We are on the brink of taking this entire gang down," he said. "Not just the chapter that was bothering your parents, but the entire structure. It's been years in the making, and we were struggling to get some headway, but the footage we have... it might help us a lot. But we will need your help."

"Okay," I said.

"You mentioned the footage of the fight," he said. "Well, we have that. I just wanted to make sure our beliefs were right about what was going on there. You see, the footage we have is a bit hard to decipher. We clearly have them in the footage, and they are clearly in the midst of a fight with several people, one of whom we believed to be you. If you are willing to testify that it was you, and that as a consequence of that fight you were blackmailed for the money we have you giving them on tape, then we could put them away."

"I don't know," I said. "I don't really want to get involved. I gave them that money so I didn't ever have to deal with them again. My family is finally done with them."

"I know," he said. "But just remember, if they are doing this to your family, they are doing the same or worse to others. You could save people's lives by testifying against them. Do you understand, son?"

"I do," I said.

"Just sleep on it, will you? Take a night to think about it, and I'll call you in the morning. Sound good?"

"Sure," I said. "Am I free to go?"

He nodded. I stood and made for the door, but before I shut it, he stopped the door, and I turned to face him.

"Just think about the other people you could help by getting these people put away, Gavin. You would be helping people just like you. People who are innocent and caught up in their web and don't have the ability to get out."

I nodded and left, my mind heavy as I headed home. By now, it was late, and stopping for burgers just wasn't going to be an option. Dinner was going to have already started by the time I got home. I pulled out my phone and saw a few calls and texts from Lila asking where I was, the last one being twenty minutes ago. I could respond, or I could just head home. Considering I was only a few blocks away, I just decided to skip the notification.

When I opened the door, I found Kevin, Emma, Lila, and Star at the table in the kitchen. I froze. Lila did not. She leaped out of her seat and ran toward me, wrapping me in a hug.

"Where have you been?" she asked.

"I have something I want to talk to you about," I said. "It's rather important."

"So do I," she said. "But first, dinner. Everything's ready, and we were just sitting down to eat."

"Okay," I said, then stopped. My eyes had fallen on a large bag, several feet tall and a couple feet wide, leaning against the wall. "What's that?"

"I have no idea," Lila said. "Star brought it. We had to turn it diagonally to get it through the door."

"Is it some kind of weapon? Are we safe?"

"I don't know what kinds of weapons are that tall, that long and that thin," she said. "But I've been listening for ticking sounds all evening and haven't heard anything. I think we're good. I think."

"Okay," I said.

"Hi, Gavin," Star said as I got to my empty seat at the table.

"Hi, Star," I said, sitting.

"Well, isn't this nice?" Emma asked. "I have pasta, sauce, some homemade garlic bread and, oh, right, the salads. Hang on."

She left the table and went to the refrigerator to retrieve a giant salad bowl. I leaned close to Kevin, who was on one side of me.

"She been like this all day?"

"I think so," Kevin said. "I had class, but when I came home, the apartment was clean."

"It was clean before," I said a bit reproachfully.

"No. It was dude-clean before. It was *clean-clean* when I came home."

As he said it, I noticed that little things around the apartment were different. For one, the closet and cabinet doors were shut all the way, a sure indication someone had been organizing. The living room looked neat, and the coffee table glass was gleaming. There was suddenly a basket that I didn't recognize sitting beside the loveseat with blankets piled in it neatly. The television was missing the thick layer of dust that had been growing since who knew when. The air also had a freshly vacuumed and candle burning scent to it, just above the herby-food smell.

"Weird," I said.

"Yeah, I don't think this is normal for her, but... it's nice?"

"What are you two whispering about?" Emma said as she returned, salad bowl in hand and beginning to dole out greens and veggies to our plates.

"Nothing," I said.

"Just how nice the place looks," Kevin said. "I noticed you did some cleaning."

Emma went red, enough that I thought she might have been suddenly holding her breath and was about to pass out, and sat down in her chair.

"It was nothing," she said, in what had to be a lie. Our place hadn't been this clean when we moved in, much less at any time since.

"Dinner smells great," Star said, reminding me again that she was here. It was so weird.

"Thanks," Emma said. "Oh, Kevin, I don't know anything about wine. Is it okay that I drank one of the bottles in the fridge?"

"Sure," he said. "That's not a pro—" He stopped and turned a little toward her. "Did you say you drank a *whole bottle*?"

"Well, not exactly," she said. "Lila had a glass and a half," she said.

"Uh huh," Lila said, sipping on what looked to be yet another glass now. "I did. This one makes two and a half."

"And we might be kind of done with the second one now, too," Emma said meekly.

Kevin laughed his trademark booming laugh.

"No wonder," he said. "I was thinking you were acting funny. Of course it's fine. I love wine, but I don't buy the expensive stuff often. Anything in the fridge is good to go. I told Gavin that if he ever wanted to bring a bottle over to St-ahh, I mean, over to Lila... and... Star's... place. Oh, shit."

"Smooth," I muttered. "Real smooth."

To my surprise, Star laughed. It was the kind of giggle that I had only ever heard the first time I met her. I always thought I had never amused her as much as that first moment.

"It's fine," Star said. "Isn't it, Lila?"

"Umm, what?" Lila asked, taking the glass away from her lips, a glass that was now suddenly devoid of most of its contents.

"I said it's fine," Star said. "We shouldn't feel awkward just because Gavin and I spent time together as a couple. We aren't together. It's fine. Right, Gavin?"

Shit, now I was being put on the spot.

"Right," I said, then cleared my throat when I heard myself sound like a teenage boy just getting into puberty. "Right. No reason to feel weird. Everything's perfectly normal."

"Well," Emma said after a moment. "Let's eat!"

"I think I need more wine," Lila said.

"Me too," Star said, her amiable smile still strapped to her face. "I really started to enjoy wine when I was on my trip. I find that it soothes my mind better than tea or coffee. I just have to be careful with it, or else I fall asleep."

"Oh how I wish I was asleep," Lila muttered.

"What was that?" Star asked.

"I said, me too," she said.

"Right," Star said. She was standing now, crossing over to the refrigerator. "Do you mind?"

The question was directed in general to both me and Kevin, and we both muttered an expression of permission. Then we looked at each other, shrugged, and did it again, louder.

"You two are so funny," Star said. "Here we go."

Star came back with the bottle, filling Lila's and then her own. When she sat down, we all slowly started in on our food, the growing awkward silence apparently affecting everyone. Everyone except for Star, who was happily bouncing as she ate.

It was also weird seeing her actually *eat*. For so long, I had watched as she consumed a stick of celery or a single apple and claimed to be full. But she was at the other end of the table from me, and I watched as she put the salad away in record time and then started in on the noodles like they would disappear if she didn't eat them fast enough. It was honestly kind of impressive.

As we ate, Kevin began regaling everyone with a story about our childhood, one that ended with one of Kevin's favorite moments in his life. The one time he beat me in a Home Run Derby when we were fifteen. His Jordan-with-a-fever dramatics of that day, having just recovered from the flu the day before, being in a mild car accident the day of, and having lost all his own bats and having to borrow mine, meant that for that one day, despite all odds, Kevin was the greatest hitter alive.

We wrapped up the food, and as I sat back, my stomach full, Star patted her lips with her napkin primly, having polished off two plates of the pasta, and gently belched.

"Holy shit," Kevin said, laughing. "Did you just burp?"

"I did," Star said, smiling. "In Japan, that's compliments to the chef."

"Accepted," Emma said, trying to withhold laughter herself.

"I just want everyone to know how happy I am to see everyone so happy," Star continued. "It really makes me ecstatic to see so many good people seemingly so content."

"Thank you," Emma said. "I'll be honest, we were a little concerned about how this was all going to come out."

"Em!" Lila whisper-yelled. Both of them had enough wine in them that their ability to be quiet was compromised, but it was kind of funny how obvious it was.

"What?" Emma said. "It's true. But it'ssall finenow," she continued, slurring her words. "Now, let me get theseplates and I'll wash'em."

"I can help!" Star said, jumping up.

"What?" Lila said, much louder than I was sure she intended.

"I thought she was notoriously messy," Kevin muttered.

"She is," Lila said, then realized how loud she was and began to whisper, "she is."

"Did I enter the Twilight Zone?" I asked. "Everyone is acting really weird."

"She never cleans anything," Lila said, shaking her head. "Now she's doing dishes? Dishes?" She hiccupped. "S'not normal."

"Let's get you into the living room. With some water," I said. "Kev, will you grab her a water bottle out of the fridge?"

I guided Lila to the living room, and when Kevin followed us with water, I cracked the bottle top and gave it to her. She drank it gratefully, and after a few minutes of Star and Emma clanging around in the kitchen, Lila started to seem like she was edging back away from drunkenness and into a less sloppy soberness.

"It's just weird," Lila said, sounding much more like herself.

"Hey, guys," Star said, coming into the room behind us. "I have something I wanted to give you. It's for you, Lila, and you, Gavin."

"Is it the giant bag?" Emma asked. "Can I help you get it out?"

"Sure," Star said, and the two of them began opening it. Slowly, Star pulled out the contents of the bag. A large canvas with an intricate and surreal painting. There were two clear figures in the painting, which was gorgeously colorful and unlike anything I had ever seen before. The figures were me and Lila. Holding hands.

"See, in the last few months, I have come to realize some things about myself," Star explained. "And about the world. When I was in France, specifically, I found out something really important. What friendship really was. And how much I needed that in my life.

"My time there, it solidified it. I was being selfish by going, and I thought the people I was with were my friends. But I was so lonely while I was there. It was beautiful, and yet, I didn't care. I just wanted to be home. I couldn't create because my mind was missing you two.

"Without friends like you, Lila, I can't do what I do. And if you two are happy together, I *want* you to be together. Because your happiness makes me happy. So when I got home, I was inspired.

"And I painted this."

Chapter Twenty-One

Lila

I WAS IN SHOCK. EMOTION flooded my body, and tears welled in my eyes. It was such a beautiful gesture, and one I didn't see coming.

"Do you like it?" Star asked.

"It's amazing," I choked out. "Oh, Star, it's wonderful."

I stood, crossing the living room to where she was waiting with open arms. To my surprise, Star began to cry on my shoulder as we hugged, and when I pulled back, she was smiling through the tears.

"I'm sorry if I can be difficult," she said. "I know I'm not the easiest person to get along with. But you are my best friend, Lila. I don't want to lose you, ever."

"I'm not going anywhere," I said.

"Good," she said, pulling me back into a tight hug. "I don't know if I could navigate this world without you."

Star didn't stay long after, making excuses to get home and get to work on a project that she had neglected while she worked on that one, and quickly made her way out. Before she did, Gavin gave her a hug, and I found myself not feeling anything negative at all. No jealousy, no worries. Only happiness. It was like a massive weight had been lifted off my shoulders.

About an hour later, with the four of us hanging out in the living room, Kevin and Emma glanced at each other, and Kevin sat forward on the seat.

"Well, I think me and Emma are going to head out," he said.

"Really?" Gavin asked. "It's like eleven. You guys hitting the club this late?"

"First off, that's not late for the clubs," Emma said, "but no, we're heading to my place for the night."

"Oh," Gavin said. "I see."

"I figured it might be nice for both couples to have a night alone," Kevin said. "Since we're all just getting used to this configuration and all. And... after... that—" He gestured vaguely to the painting and the dining room table.

"It was an interesting night, for sure," Gavin said. "I don't want to feel like you have to leave on account of us, though."

"We're not," Emma said. "The plan has been to go to my place tonight since this morning. I need to water my plants and stuff, and Kevin left some things there."

"All right, well, I guess we'll see you guys tomorrow?" I asked.

"We have practice," Emma said. "So, yeah, you'll see me."

"Same for us," Kevin said. "We could all go out or something tomorrow evening."

"That might be fun," I said. "Do you think we should invite Star?"

The four of us looked at each other and collectively shrugged.

"We'll play that by ear, but I don't mind," Gavin said.

"Us either," Emma said, speaking for Kevin. "Tonight was weird, but I think it'd be better next time."

A round of hugs and goodbyes later and they were out of the door, leaving Gavin and me alone.

As Gavin locked the door behind them, I went to the kitchen and got both of us another glass of wine. I was fully sober now, but I knew we had some things to talk about before bed and wanted to make sure I had the liquid courage to do so. Besides, the bottle was almost empty anyway. I was just saving refrigerator space, right?

"So," Gavin said as he sat down beside me, "which one of us goes first?"

"Rock, paper, scissors?" I suggested.

Gavin laughed. "Or I could just let you go first," he said. "Go on. Let's hear your big news."

I took a deep breath. *Here goes nothing.* I told him about what Coach said about being invited to join a national team, and what that meant of trying out for the Olympics.

"It would be a big time sink," I said. "But it's everything I've worked for in softball my entire life. Playing in the Olympics would be a dream, and Coach thinks I have a really good shot at making the team. Especially if I play well on the traveling team. Plus, I'd get to see a bit of the world and go places I might not ever get a chance to otherwise."

"Of course," he said.

"But that means that I will essentially be gone for like a year," I said. "I know we just started... this. But how would we navigate that and do it from such a distance? I don't want to hold you back. If you would be happier dating other people..."

"Stop right there," he said, pulling my hands into his lap and turning toward me. "I need you to listen to me."

"Okay," I said.

"I do not want to date anyone else," he said. "I mean it. I don't want anyone but you. If that's too much for *you*, let me know, but I am perfectly willing to play everything by ear and see you when I can see you."

I nearly burst into tears.

"Really?" I asked, trying desperately to hold back the emotion. By the warble in my voice, I was failing miserably.

"Yes," he said. "I am so proud of you."

As he pulled me into a tight hug, I let the tears flow. There was no sobbing, no hitching breath, just tears that seemed to be pulling all the sadness, all the anxiety, all the worry out of my body and washing it away. With every tear, I felt lighter, happier, and more in control.

"I am incredibly proud of you," he reiterated. "And I will be there for you when you get back. We can see each other in the middle. We will be able to work it out. I know we can. I know this relationship is new, but it kind of isn't at the same time, right? It's not like we just met. I feel like I've been in love with you for months, and I just let it all out. This is going to just be the way it is."

"I feel the same way," I said. "I just worried you didn't."

"I do," he said. "I absolutely do."

He smiled, and I pressed my lips to his for a kiss. When I pulled away, he handed me a tissue from a box Emma must have placed on the coffee table because I had never seen one at his place before. As I wiped away tears, I folded my legs under me on the couch and tried to compose myself.

"All right," I said, feeling like I was in a small measure of control again. "So what's your news?"

He let out a long breath and sighed. "So I got a call from a detective from Myrtle Beach today," he began. As he filled me in on what the detective told him and the plan for him to testify, I couldn't believe it. It sounded like it was going to be a major case and that even Kevin, Emma, and I might get dragged into it at some point.

"I just want you to know," I said, "I will be there for you as much as I can. Any time you have to testify, anything, if I can work it out, I will be there. And if they need to speak to me, I am open for that too."

He smiled. "Good," he said. "Maybe we can put those bastards away for good." He took a sip of his wine and then put down the glass on a coaster that was also somehow brand new and ancient. It looked like it was from the seventies and yet had never been used. "Now aside from all that, I think I've come to a decision about my career. I think I am going to enter the draft a year early and see what happens. My scholarship money is all dried up, and I didn't really do much to impress at the tournament, so I was thinking I should participate in the draft camp."

"You mean this year?" I asked.

He nodded. "Yeah," he said. "It might work out really well too. If you are traveling with the national team, and I get picked up and enter the minors, we might crisscross a couple of times."

"That would be fun," I said. "I'd love that for you."

"I think it might be the way to go," he said. "I'm going to think on it a little more, and I'm going to talk to Coach about it, but if I can impress at draft camp, I might get a signing bonus from whoever picks me up that could at least pay the bills for a while."

"If you think you should do it, then we will figure it out. We will figure it all out," I said.

He grinned.

For the rest of the night, we talked. Plans for how we would see each other in between series if we could, even talk about the possibility of finding a place together if we felt comfortable with that later on. It was all so tentative, but at the same time not. We already knew how much we were stuck on each other and had been for so long. The idea of jumping into the deep waters of a serious relationship wasn't as crazy as it theoretically should have been.

Like he'd said, we weren't strangers. We knew each other quite well, had spent a lot of time together both alone and with other people. And we were clearly very compatible in the bedroom.

Extremely so.

So it wasn't that far of a stretch to think that if we were still going strong like we both thought we would be, then when he was home for the offseason and I was in between tours in the fall and winter, that we might find a place together. It wasn't a big dramatic 'move in with me' statement, but more of a casual acknowledgement that if things continued, we would face that possibility rather quickly. And neither of us balked.

It was getting late, and we were both yawning, trying to stay awake as we talked through each other's exciting opportunities, and when I found myself dozing off on the couch, Gavin beckoned me to go to bed with him.

He could have made me feel guilty about not being intimate since we had the house to ourselves, but he didn't. Instead, he offered me one of his T-shirts to sleep in, which I took gratefully, knowing full well I had pajamas in my bag, and prepared a space for me in the bed next to him.

It was strangely comforting to go through a nighttime routine with him. We stood side by side as we brushed our teeth, and when I shut the door of the bathroom to change, it didn't feel weird. When I came out in his T-shirt, I knew it excited him, but he could tell how tired I was. There was no pressure.

Everything was easy.

I crawled into his arms and found the nook that I had discovered I fit in so well while we were at the beach. He had turned on a little box fan, not for the air but for the sound, and the white noise drowned out everything else. It didn't take long before I was falling into a happy, contented sleep.

When morning came, I awoke before he did and blinked a few times. My nose was buried in his chest, and I took in the scent of him giddily. He was wearing one of his T-shirts too and a pair of boxers. A pair of boxers that were noticeably tented in the early morning hours.

Deviously, I grinned at the possibility presenting itself to me, and with all the stress off my mind and a good night's rest, I was feeling like waking up Gavin. In a very special way.

I kissed his chest, and he shifted in his sleep. Slowly, I made my way down his chest to his stomach with my kisses, and as I reached the edge of his boxers, I felt him shift again, and the weight of his head rising and falling back on the pillow.

Reaching into the opening of his boxers, I found his hardened cock. I stroked him as I slipped him out of his boxers, and he groaned deeply. I looked up to see his eyes, open but groggy, staring down at me.

A smile was stretching across his face. Greedily, I smiled back as I ran my tongue along the underside of him and relished the sound of his moan.

I took him into my lips and let his cock slide down into my throat, loving the warm, massive member on my tongue. He clearly appreciated it too, as his body tensed and his cock hardened even more. Bobbing up and down, I sucked him, my hand stroking him into my mouth with every time I came up. He groaned loudly, and I increased my speed. Even if it this was all that was going to happen this morning, I was happy.

I just wanted to pleasure him.

Chapter Twenty-Two

Gavin

HER LIPS WRAPPED AROUND me almost had me emptying myself already. I pulled her up, and she crawled up my body, letting her lips brush my skin on my stomach and chest. I met her as she climbed over, straddling me. I needed her. I needed to be in her.

The stresses and worries I had been feeling in my mind were gone. Now all that mattered was her. I pulled at the T-shirt, and she lifted her arms to let it come up and off her. Tossing it away, my hands slid up her stomach and to her breasts, filling with them and kneading into them. She moaned as she ground her core over my cock. Her panties were wet and thin, and my cock slid through her folds, tantalizingly close but blocked by the fabric.

I let one hand slide down her to her panties and pushed them aside, revealing her soft hair and wet lips. She gasped as I revealed her, and she slid her body up to cover my staff with her juices. Back and forth she rocked, my head pressing against her clit and making her cry out. Then she pushed her hips up, and I pushed my cock into her soft folds. I slid inside.

"Oh, Gavin," she said as I entered her.

Slowly, she lowered until I filled her, and she let her hands fall back on the bed, her jaw locked open in ecstasy. My thumb swirled over her clit as she rode me, and I watched as her breasts rose and fell faster and faster as she breathed heavily and moaned. Her hips rocked hard and fast, and my thumb pressed in. Suddenly, she pressed down until my cock was completely buried in her, and her body shook. Her toes curled, and her voice trailed off in a weak gasp.

I pulled her down by her hips and then rolled, pushing her down into the bed on her back. Her thighs were still shaking, and she was biting her bottom lip as I mounted her. I curled into her, wrapping one arm over her head and holding her still as I kissed her while my hips began to slam into her. Her moans came quick and sharp, and her eyes clenched shut as she wrapped her legs around me.

Nails dug into my back as I felt her squeezing, climbing the mountain of another climax and falling off again. When she released me, she fell back onto the bed, her eyes burning into mine and her hands falling by the side of her head. I clasped them by the wrist and pressed down, planking over her as my cock buried deep inside her pussy.

Lila begged for more, and I gave her everything I had. I was slamming into her with abandon, her legs raised high to give me better access. I felt myself about to explode. I pulled her hands up over her head and kissed her deeply. My head fell down by her neck, and I could hear her moans so loudly that it filled every bit of sound in the room to me.

"Come for me," she begged. "Please, Gavin, come for me."

My body locked solid as I slammed into her one last time. I felt the intense, mind-blowing orgasm with my entire body, tingling from the top of my head down through my toes. I emptied into her in bursts, and she moaned in satisfaction with each one.

Finally spent, I fell into her arms, and both of us began to laugh. It was a joyous laugh, and as I kissed her skin until our lips met again, neither of us could wipe the smile from our faces. I rolled onto my back, and she curled into me.

I had never felt as happy in my entire life as I did in that moment.

Three Months Later...

"All right, Mr. Freeman. Can you raise your right hand and repeat after me?"

The first few moments were like a dream. It didn't feel real. Lila and I had watched hundreds of hours of court depositions to try and prepare me for what it would be like up there. Kevin had even helped do a mock trail so I could get used to testifying as a witness, with him acting as the defense attorney. I felt as prepared as I could possibly be, and yet, it was still terrifying.

As I sat down in the chair, I stared across the room into the eyes of the three men I'd had a fistfight with that night in Myrtle Beach. In the light of the courtroom, they looked so much less intimidating. Perhaps it was the bright orange jumpsuits, but for some reason, they didn't bother me nearly as much as the fear of doing something wrong and them getting off on a technicality based on my statements.

I just needed to breathe and tell the truth.

My eyes shifted over to the gallery, where Lila, Kevin, Emma, and even Star were sitting. Beside Lila was also one other person I never expected to be there for me. My mother. The seat was elevated, enough that I could see that she and Lila were holding hands.

Mom had been in rehab for two months and had called me when she arrived at her aunt's house not long after that. Aunt Patsy had kept her on the straight and narrow ever since, and Mom was looking healthier than I had ever seen her. Her hair was cut short, just below her ears, and styled. In my life, I had only ever seen it down, hanging with loose ends around her shoulders, or piled in a ponytail or braids.

For the last week, she had been back in town in Georgia. She had gotten a remote job, and as long as she had her laptop, she could work, meaning she was able to stay in a vacation house nearby and be with us for the trial. Her own testimony had happened the day before, and I had never been prouder of her than I was when she faced the bastards down and told the jury exactly what they had done.

Kevin had also testified yesterday, though his testimony was rather short. During cross, they only had asked him if he was sure of the men there were the ones he fought, since he knew nothing of why the fight started. When he pointed them out, he mentioned that the bearded one still bore the scar that Kevin gave him. That's how he was sure.

Now it was my turn. I tried to be as brave as my mother and Kevin and look them in the eye when I spoke. I told the truth. I didn't hesitate to talk about the reasons why they would have such leverage, and my mother seemed to take it in stride. Enough that when I glanced over at her, she simply nodded at me, a thin smile on her face. It was ugly, telling the world who we had been, but it was worth it.

We took a recess, and I went out to the hall with them. My stomach was churning, but I was still, somehow, hungry.

"Maybe we should grab a sandwich or something while we have this break," I said.

"Well, about that," Kevin said. "I have a surprise for you."

"A surprise?" I asked. "At court?"

"Sort of," he said.

Walking away, he came back moments later, surrounded by a group of people I knew very well.

"Holy shit, it's the whole freaking team," I said.

"Wow," Lila said. "Emma, did you know about this?"

"I did!" she said. "I kept a secret for once!"

About fourteen of my teammates had made the trip to South Carolina, plus three of the coaches. They surrounded me, shaking my hand and giving me high-fives.

"We didn't want to come in during the first part of your testimony," Raul said. "So we all got lunch for you guys. Come on. We have a room next door."

The building next door was a hybrid space, one where lawyers and their clients could meet and strategize while also being able to crash if they needed to. Multiple tiny offices and several open office spaces allowed anyone to work there or have meetings for various purposes. In the largest private room, one that was clearly used for corporate presentations, the team had gathered a spread of pizzas, sodas, and burgers. Classic ballplayer food.

We dug in as we sat and tried to relax a little. We were due back in court in two hours, but that was plenty of time to chill out a bit and get some food in us. As I was digging into my third slice, Emma flicked me in the arm and got my attention.

"Hey, isn't that your mom with Coach Williams?"

"She's looking very chummy with him," Kevin said.

"Well, I'll be," I said. "Coach just got divorced, didn't he?"

"Yeah, he made us do extra running drills the week his wife ran off with some dude. Angry as fuck that week," Raul said. "He chilled out afterwards, though. Hell of a pitching coach."

"He is," I said. "Good for them."

Lila giggled a little.

"Good for them," she repeated.

"Well, the idea was to show you that no matter how crap-tacular your family might end up being, you always had a family in us," Bryant, one of the centerfielders and a long-time teammate of mine dating back to high school said. "But now it looks like it might become kind of literal."

"They're just talking," Kevin said. "Leave them be."

"Good for them," I repeated, shaking my head and digging back into my pizza. "I just want you guys to know that I am touched you came. I appreciate this."

"For sure," Dante said. "We've got your back."

"What he said," Chris chimed in.

"Thanks, guys," I said. "You have no idea how much this helps."

A few weeks later, the smaller group of us were together again. Emma and Kevin, Mom, Lila, and I stood as the jury rose to give their verdict. Lila was between my mother and me and was holding both our hands. When the judge asked if the jury was unanimous in their decision, and they affirmed it, I felt like I was going to be sick to my stomach.

Then they read the verdict. Guilty.

Assault. Battery. Extortion. Drug offenses. The whole nine yards. They were looking at the rest of their lives in prison. As we exited the courthouse, elated and joyously tearful, Detective Eudy made his way over, hand extended for a shake. I took it firmly, and he pulled me in for a quick bro-hug.

"This is the first of the dominos to fall," he said. "I've heard from the prosecutor that they are already looking for a plea deal to make things better on themselves. They're willing to sing about the entire operation. The whole syndicate is going to come down, and it is because of you, Kevin, and you Gavin. Especially your testimony. If it weren't for that, I honestly don't know if we would be able to pin them on anything else. Your testimony linked everything together."

"I'm just happy to do my part," I said.

"Well, you did that and then some," he said. "You have my card. When you get drafted, let me know. I want to see you play."

"Sure," I said. "And it's *if* I get drafted," I said.

"Pshh," Kevin said. "You know better than that. You've got two weeks until the combine. You've been tossing fire and hitting bombs. You're a lock."

"My agent thinks so," I said. "I just don't know."

"You have an agent already?" Eudy asked.

"Yeah," I said. "Coach Williams. He played a decade ago. Got a taste of the Show for two seasons with the Cubs. He's been guiding me through this."

"He's a good man," Mom said, and I rolled my eyes.

"He is, Mom," I agreed. "He still treating you good?"

"He's been a perfect gentleman, if that's what you're asking," she said.

I laughed.

With this chapter of my life over, it really felt like I was on the precipice of something else. My hands linked in Lila's, I was ready to take those steps. Wherever they might lead. One place in particular, I was pretty damn sure of. But that would have to wait. Just a little while longer.

Chapter Twenty-Three

Lila

THE DRAFT BEING MOVED to July from June meant an extra month of preparation for Gavin. He used every single bit of that time to work out hard and build his strength and stamina up while I finished up the first half of the national team season. The combine had gone extremely well for him, and Coach Williams said his slot was looking like a second-round pick, but there were rumors he might end up in the first round, and rather early, by a team that needed a player like him and were willing to overlook the Spring tournament after the trial. The excitement in his voice when he told me that was adorable and infectious.

With the college season finally ended, Breyer University ending up winning a pennant and playing in the semi-final round of the playoffs before being eliminated. Gavin was able to show off even more in high pressure situations. While the team didn't make it, his individual performance was the best of his career. I could only hope it would lead to a big draft bonus with a team ready to make something out of him. He just wanted to play baseball.

Meanwhile, my national team success was almost boring. I tried out with the teams and did extremely well with the various squads in pre-season. We were outplaying every team we came across and mowing them down. I had been converted full-time to a pitcher, working on my mechanics, and the team choosing not to use a designated hitter when I was on the mound. But not getting to play in the field every day was starting to weigh on me, and I was working up the courage to ask Coach to let me play one of the corner spots when I wasn't throwing.

Still, I knew that the final cuts were coming, and I had only days before I would know if I made the team or not. Both Gavin and I were going to be playing the waiting game by the phone to find out at the same time. But we had already made a pact. No matter what happened, we were going to make it work. We would find a way.

Because we were in love.

It was thrilling just to be able to say that to myself, much less directly to him. We weren't going to let anything interfere with our love, and in the meantime, we were going to go spend the downtime before the roster announcements and his draft by spending time together.

It started with coming home and spending an entire week in the apartment. Kevin and Emma made themselves scarce for the week, which meant that Gavin and I didn't really bother to wear clothes for days. It was glorious. But now, we were at least going to have to wear a few of them, as the vacation turned from being one of just us to being with family.

My family.

In Myrtle Beach.

The drive over was its own adventure. I had told him all about the family, including Mom and my uncle who owned the house, who had decided to let Mom have the keys while he went to Tahiti for the summer. How it had sparked a family argument about not everyone being there, and how Mom was convinced that he would just come back for a few days while the rest of the family was in his house, 'for the sake of family.'

The quizzes Gavin put himself through on the drive were funny, but I knew he was actually stressing about it. At least he was only going to have to deal with my female cousins. The boys were with my uncle on a beach. Far away from Mom.

As Gavin liked to say, good for them.

We pulled into the beach house at almost noon, and I told him to leave the bags in the car. There was no way we were going to make it to our room anytime soon. Sure enough, when we knocked on the door, we were bombarded by my cousins, their tiny children, and of course, my mother.

"Lila, it's about time you made it," Mom said in a tone that could sound silly and joking to people who didn't know her, but I knew was deadly serious. "Come in, come in. Lunch is getting cold."

"Oh, we already ate," I said.

"Of course you did. Everyone eats breakfast. But lunch is ready now. Your cousin Theresa made it."

"It's taramasalata," Theresa said. "From scratch."

Gavin stepped in behind me, and I watched as all my cousins faces went white and my mother stopped chopping a cucumber in mid-swipe.

"So, everyone, this is Gavin. He's my boyfriend."

"Hello, everyone," he said. "Thanks for having me."

"You've got to be kidding me," Arianna, another of my cousins, mumbled. Her husband was six feet away from her and glanced over, then saw Gavin, then rolled his eyes.

Mom stepped from behind the counter, leaving a half-chopped cucumber in her wake, something she never did because she either never wanted to be part of any cooking process, and when she did, she was deadly serious about it. She stepped up to Gavin and offered her hand. There was something in her expression I could barely make out because I had never seen it before. Then it clicked.

She was impressed.

"Hello, Gavin," she said. "I am Tati, Lila's mother. I've heard so much about you. I must say the pictures she sent me do not do you justice."

If Gavin wasn't directly behind me, the strength of the eyeroll I just had would have knocked me over backwards. She was, in one sentence, able to insult me by insinuating I didn't properly talk about how gorgeous he was, give him the nickname that only my father uses, and slyly kind of hit on him. It was a triple whammy.

"Nice to meet you," Gavin said, clearly lying. "Babe, shall I go get our stuff?"

"No, no, come eat first," Mom said. "A big strong boy like you must need to eat, what, ten times a day?"

She had taken Gavin by the arm and was walking away with him. He looked back with a sad, panicked look on his face, to which I could only shrug. I'd tried to warn him. She was going to stuff him full of food, while casually mentioning that if I laid off the bread, I might look better in my swimsuit. That was how this week was going to go. At least the parts of it we were going to spend with them.

Arianna appeared at my side almost instantly, watching Gavin walk into the kitchen with Mom and a couple of the other cousins.

"Fucking hell, Lila," she said.

"Your mama lets you talk like that now?" I asked with a grin.

"You tell her, and I punch your lip," she said, an ancient threat dating back to the days when we were both in pre-school. Arianna was the closest to me in age and was unfairly pretty. Taking the most of the good Greek genes in our family, she had thick, brown, curly hair and tanned skin. Giant boobs and a tiny waist meant she looked like a model, always, and her husband, Frank, was well aware that she knew exactly how lucky Frank was that he'd knocked her up when she was eighteen.

"I won't say a word," I said.

"He is *beautiful,*" she said. "Your mom said he's a baseball player."

"Yup. The draft is in a few days. We figured some time away at the beach would be good for relaxing before he finds that out and I find out if I made the national softball team."

"Look at you," Arianna said, elbowing my arm. "Living the dream. I'm jealous. I'd climb that man like a tree."

"I do, often," I said, feeling my cheeks burn as Arianna turned slowly to me, her jaw open and a giant laugh rumbling from her chest.

"You're bad. I like it. I'll need details later. With alcohol."

"Lila," Mom called from the kitchen, "I have the extra bedroom set up for Gavin. If you could be a dear and make sure he has some towels in there. The linen closet is full, right between your rooms."

"Um, that won't be necessary," I said. "He's going to be sleeping with me."

There was a hush that fell over the room, and the burning in my cheeks was now taking over every other part of my body. I felt like I was on fire, and yet, I wasn't going to shrivel up or back off. There was no way I was going to let my mother's prudishness and self-righteousness keep me from Gavin this week. Not a chance.

"Lila, dear. You two aren't even engaged. I think everyone would feel more comfortable if..."

"I am an adult, Mother," I said. "And Gavin will be staying with me. If that won't work for you, we could always get a hotel down the street."

Mom's eyes burned into mine for a moment, and I could feel the apoplectic shitfit she was about to throw. Then, suddenly, it went away. She backed off.

"No, that's fine. You're right, of course. You are an adult. As long as Gavin is fine with that arrangement."

"Sleeping with Lila? Yes. It's one of my favorite activities."

The laughter that emanated from Arianna was so loud, so distracting, that I barely even noticed how hard everyone else was laughing too. Even Frank was guffawing. Through teary eyes, I held on to the wall, shaking with laughter myself, and when I finally looked back up, even Mom was chuckling.

"Walked right into that one," she said. "Fine then. Frank, will you help them get their things?"

A few days on the beach was just what I needed. I could feel the stress sliding off of me, and with my mother's newfound inability to get under my skin, it was even better. There was a confidence I had now, with Gavin beside me, that let me just ignore her when she got going. And she got going a lot less, too, which helped.

Each day seemed to be building to something, though, and I didn't know what. I had a feeling we were going to get the call from the national team coach while we were there, but it felt like perhaps there was something else too. Some shoe was about to drop. I could feel it.

The night before the draft arrived, and Gavin and I were hanging out in the living room when I got a call on my phone. It was the national team coach. I was in.

The celebration in the house was intense. My family, perhaps for the first time, seemed to accept me as the person I was. They were finally willing to celebrate me and my accomplishments, even if they weren't what they'd hoped for for me. Drinks were flowing, and everyone was enjoying the moment when Gavin snuck up behind me and wrapped his arms around my waist. Most of the family was either downstairs with the pool table and drinking or having already found somewhere to fall asleep.

"Excuse me," he said. "I have somewhere we need to go."

I laughed as he lifted me easily, carrying me through the house and out of the double doors that led to the beach. I was still wearing a white sundress over my bikini, and the light wind picked it up and pushed it beyond my knees. I saw Gavin take a quick glance as he made his way down sand dunes to the water. Then he kept walking,

"When are you putting me down?" I asked.

"When we get over here," he said, nodding to a spot in the beach that was surrounded by rocks. A secluded place I had shown him a day before. A thrill went up my spine. I now had a feeling I knew what he was thinking.

A recreation of our night on the beach all those months ago. Only this time, I wasn't going to be running anywhere.

He put me down on the soft sand and pulled out a blanket from a bag I didn't even realize he was carrying over his shoulder. He laid it down on the beach and then took my hands in his. Slowly, we went to our knees, and his lips pressed into mine.

"Want to pick up where we left off that night?"

"More than you will ever know," I said.

I pulled up on the sundress, letting it go over my head and exposing my bikini-clad body to the night. He yanked at his shirt and then pulled off his shorts, revealing the same pair of trunks he had been wearing that night. I laughed and then mounted him, pulling his face to mine and letting our lips touch.

This time there was no hesitancy. No need to run away. I was his. He was mine. And what we were going to do on that secluded portion of the beach was exactly what was right.

Chapter Twenty-Four

Gavin

SOMEHOW, LILA WAS EVEN more beautiful than she had ever been. With the stars in the sky above her, the sound of the waves crashing on the sand nearby, the seclusion of the rocks keeping us private while also being out on the private beach, it was a sensory overload. And I wanted more.

I pulled at the string of her bikini bottom. It unraveled easily, and I reached to do the same on the other side. It fell on my stomach, revealing her wet pussy to me, and I pulled the fabric up and out of the way. I tossed it over to the sundress and reached for her top. It unraveled easily, and she pulled her shoulders together to let it drop off her and into my hands.

She was naked. Completely nude under the moonlight. I aimed to join her immediately.

But first, she slid down my legs, her eyes still focused on mine as she reached down and grabbed my shorts. As she pulled them down, she slowly revealed my throbbing, thick cock. It sprang out, and she laughed in delight before pulling the shorts completely off me. Now we were both naked, and she took my cock in her hand and brought her lips down to it.

I groaned as she took me into her mouth, but I wasn't satisfied with just letting her do the work. I pulled on her thigh until she moved herself over and climbed over my head. I slid my tongue through her folds, and she cried out, the vibration of her voice on my cock and sending shivers across my body.

I licked her, swirling the tip of my tongue over her clit until she was moaning and bobbing her head up and down on my staff. Sliding a finger inside her froze her for a moment as she was blinded by the sensation. I let the pad of my finger brush the top of her wall while I focused on sliding my tongue over her pearl. Her body was locking still. She was close already. Her hips pushed back, and her toes curled. She shoved my cock deep in her mouth and began to shake.

She came, and I reveled in how I could make her body tremble. When she regained a measure of control of herself, she scooted down, and I sat up, rolling her to her side and curling around her. She lifted one leg, and I slid one of mine between hers, the head of my cock pressing against her opening. One arm was around her, and I filled my hand with her breast as I penetrated her, sliding deep inside her pussy.

There was cream on my cock from her climax, and I slowly thrust into her, harder each time while our lips met again. My free hand slid between her thighs and over her clit, causing her to cry out. Gently, I swirled over her as I fucked her from behind, and her hand grasped my bicep, squeezing hard as I increased the speed. Her voice warbled, one note being shaken as I slammed into her.

She turned her face to mine. Her eyes were pleading, begging for release.

"Are you going to come for me, baby?" I asked.

She nodded.

"Come for me," I grumbled. "I want you to come."

Her cry was so loud, I was sure someone would have heard us as she clenched and I thrust with big, deep slams. I was getting close myself, but I wanted to dominate her first. To smother her and show her that she was mine. I climbed between her thighs as she shook, her body weak as her arms lay by her side. I folded her in half, her feet almost at her ears as I mounted her again.

My hands dug into the sand as I rocked into her with a furious abandon. Her eyes rolled to the back of her head as she moaned softly. Her thighs occasionally shook, and I increased the speed until I felt I was going to explode. I kissed her deeply and she opened her eyes to focus on me. She begged for me to release. She wanted it.

She always did.

I gritted my teeth as I pounded her, and letting out a roar, I emptied myself. I filled her until she was dripping with my essence and collapsed into her arms. Panting, I rolled to my back, and she snuggled into my arm. We caught our breath as the waves rushed the beach and the sky twinkled above.

For quite some time, we lay there, her sundress pulled over us as a makeshift blanket, and watched the stars. There was a contentment in the moment unlike anything else I had ever experienced. I knew what I was going to do. It was time. This was the last thing that I needed to set right before I could. One last thing I needed to do to make sure it was still what I wanted.

For months, the image of that night on the beach had haunted me. A part of me was scared to move forward, thinking that I would always be chasing the high of that night and trying to fix the heartbreak that followed. But now, with her naked body pressed against mine on the very same beach, just miles from where we had been, I knew that it wasn't the case. I wanted her then. I wanted her now. And I would want her forever.

"We should get dressed," I said.

She whimpered and moaned, and I laughed.

"I don't want to," she said childishly. "I want to stay naked here on this beach with you forever."

"Ahh, yes, but imagine how nice a shower will feel to get this sand off us."

"Will you shower with me?" she asked.

"Of course," I said.

"And then we can have round two?"

"Any time you want," I said, lifting her chin with my finger and pressing a kiss to her lips.

"Fiiiine," she said, tossing the sundress off her and sitting up.

"I don't think I will ever get tired of seeing your body without a stitch of clothing on," I said.

"Same goes for you," she said, leaning down and pressing a kiss to my cock. It stirred, and I laughed.

"Trying to wake him up already?"

She shrugged, a devious smile on her face.

We stood, gathering our clothes and putting them back on, checking the area to see if there was anyone out there spying on us. When we felt like we were good to go, we snuck out of our rock enclosure and headed back to the beach. I had the back around one shoulder and her hand in the other until we reached the water. She took off ahead of me and dipped her feet in, and I followed beside her.

"I love the water when it's warm," she said.

"It's pretty great," I said. My hand slipped inside the bag and grabbed the tiny box inside the zippered portion that most people stuck their phones in. I quickly got it into my shorts before she turned to look at me and then back to look at the ocean.

"The way it looks at night... there's nothing like this. I think, maybe, one day, I might want to move out here."

"Me too," I said. "Myrtle Beach specifically has a lot of memories for me."

"Not all of them great," she laughed.

"No, but the ones that are great outweigh the ones that aren't by a lot."

She looked back at me, tucking her chin into her shoulder shyly and blinking her big, beautiful eyelashes at me. She was so pretty. So perfect. Why didn't I see it earlier? Why didn't I listen to myself?

Oh well. I had her now. It was time. If there ever was a time, it was now.

We walked a few more steps in the soft, wet sand.

“I want you to know I am extremely proud of you for making the team,” I said. “I know you are going to kill it and make the Olympics.”

“I hope so,” she said. “But either way, I know that you will be supporting me, and you have such a big day tomorrow...” She stopped, suddenly realizing I wasn’t directly beside her anymore. Turning, she looked behind and then down to where I was kneeling in the sand.

In my hand, I had the open box. The ring shone in the starlight. It was every dollar I had left in my savings, and I had a line of credit for the rest, but from what I heard from Coach, my signing bonus was going to take care of it and then a lot more.

Her breath hitched. She froze.

“Lila, I love you. I will love you forever. I know that. You are my family. The one person I can trust, who knows me for me and loves me for it anyway. Just as I love you. Part of me didn’t want to do this tonight, to overshadow your news. But at the same time, in this twilight between the biggest nights of both our lives, I felt like it couldn’t possibly be a better time to promise you that no matter what, our bond is going nowhere.

“Lila, will you do me the honor of marrying me?”

“Yes,” she choked out. “Yes, yes, Hell yes!”

I smiled, harder than I ever had, as I took the ring out of the box and slipped it on her trembling finger. Then I stood, and she collapsed into me, her lips pressing against mine and her arms wrapping tightly around me. I picked her up again, carrying her along the beach as she kissed my cheeks, my neck, my forehead.

“I want to tell everyone!” she said.

“It’s late. Are you sure?” I asked.

“Yes!”

Inside, there were still a few people up, and when she saw them, she ran to them, holding out her finger and showing them the ring. Her cousin Arianna was the first one to see it, followed by her mother and father. The celebration that had died down from earlier kicked back up again. Adults came from their bedrooms in various states of drunken or sober slumber to join in the festivities.

We partied until four in the morning, dancing, singing, rejoicing in Lila and me, and the bond we were creating.

But as everyone else finally found resting places both in their rooms and on various couches and chairs around the house, Lila took my hand and guided me to our room. As the door shut behind me, she took off the sundress and set it aside. Then, slowly, she undid her bikini, letting it fall to the floor before crawling delicately into the bed.

I watched her with a smirk.

When she was under the covers, I took off my shirt, then my shorts, letting my thick, erect cock spring out again. I was ready for round two. I thought I always would be.

"Come here, fiancé," she said. "It's been four whole hours since we got engaged, and you haven't been intimate with me yet."

"What a terrible thing," I said with a grin. "I have to remedy that, right away."

I climbed into the bed, immediately kissing her and settling between her thighs. As my cock slid into her, she gasped, just like the first time and every time since. I smiled and took her breast in my mouth. I would never tire of hearing her pleasure. Of giving her pleasure. Of being pleasured by her.

We made love until the sun rose over the blue ocean and collapsed in sweat and satisfaction to slumber until noon. Breakfast would wait. Lunch would wait. Nothing would be more important than our bodies entwined and the sound of the ocean through the open window.

It was paradise.

Chapter Twenty-Five

Lila

IN SIX MONTHS, EVERYTHING had changed.

I was engaged to the most wonderful man on Earth, a first-round draftee in the major leagues, and a man who loved me with every inch of his being. He worshipped me in the same way that I worshipped him. And time and space were not going to keep us apart.

We were standing at the airport. I had a ticket in my hand, bags at my feet, and everything I needed all either on my person or packed away. Well, everything except for Gavin.

I was off to tour with the national team, playing both third base and pitching, giving me a chance to impress on both fronts and a higher chance of making the Olympic team. The new year was starting with me traveling to the Dominican Republic for three weeks to tour there. Meanwhile, Gavin was going to be heading to Spring Training for rookie level ball in Augusta. Being drafted by Atlanta meant he didn't have to move yet, which would make seeing each other easier.

"Are you ready?" he asked after the flight was announced as boarding.

"No," I said. "I don't know how I could be. I don't want to leave you."

"I know," he said. "I don't want you to go either. But this is important. It's your dream. You have to chase it. And I'm not going anywhere. You know that."

"Yes, but six weeks and some change of not sleeping in the same bed as you," I said. "I don't know how I can handle that."

"You have my pillow," he said. "You have several of my T-shirts. And we have phones with video calling capabilities. You can make a mock me and stick the phone on the head, and we can make it through."

"I love you," I said, laughing and shaking my head. "I love you so much."

"And I love you. Now go get on the plane before you are relegated to a middle seat."

"Okay," I said, reluctantly, reaching down for one of my bags.

"Oh, I forgot to tell you," he said. I cocked an eyebrow.

"What?" I asked.

"I might, maybe have found out that my schedule would allow me to come down for the last week of your games. Including the award ceremony. Because you guys are winning that tournament."

"Really?!" I shouted far too loudly in an airport to not get the attention of very serious men in very serious suits. "You are going to come see me?"

He nodded, grinning wide.

"I wouldn't miss it. You just play your ass off. Well, not all of your ass. I am very, very fond of your ass."

"I know," I said, grinning myself. "Do you want to smack it one more time before I go?"

"Yes," he said, promptly, then whacked me with his palm on my backside. I knew it was silly, but I loved when he did that. He did too.

"Okay," he said. "Go. Get on the plane. I'll see you in about five weeks."

"I love you," I said, kissing him again. "I'll call you tonight."

"I'll be waiting," he said.

With that, I turned my back, looking over my shoulder so many times that I nearly tripped twice, and headed to the plane. As it taxied away a half hour later, I waved to the terminal, convincing myself he could see me even though I couldn't see him. When the plane took to the air, I closed my eyes, put in my earbuds, and turned on the track I'd been waiting to play. One of my favorite books as an audio book.

Read by Gavin.

He had taken weeks to make it for me, just for the trip, and I sighed as I heard his voice start to read the pages. A tear fell across my cheek. I wiped it away and felt the engagement ring brush my face. I looked down at it and smiled.

We were going to make this work.

No matter what.

Epilogue

Gavin

Two Years Later

SMACK.

The sound of the ball hitting the glove that hard was satisfying. Sure, the catcher wasn't Kevin, but Mikie was a good dude, and one of the best defensive catchers in the league. He was going to take care of me. I could feel it.

Most players were still in double-A or triple-A ball after two years, but the Ohtani effect had them grasping for players like myself. On just the third game of the season, I was called up. One of the guys in the rotation was going down for Tommy John surgery, opening up a roster spot and a rotation spot. I was going to get to fill it.

The first meeting with my new coach was enlightening. He believed in me. He had seen my games in the minors and lots of tape. He knew I could hang in the big leagues. If I stuck to my mechanics, I was going to get a shot to start every fifth day from the mound, and three days a week, I was going to get a chance somewhere on the field as a positional player. I wasn't going to play a hundred and sixty-two, but I'd play a lot. If I could keep up.

Smack.

The last of the warm-up pitches hit the glove with a satisfying sound and I tipped my cap to Mikie as he jogged over to me. It was time. The sounds of the game were loud, and the crowd even louder. There was a lot of buzz about my debut. The stands were packed in Atlanta.

The bullpen door opened, and I jogged out onto the field, doing what I could to keep my emotions in check. I was jogging through a major league field, heading to the mound. It was everything I had ever worked for. Just about everything I ever wanted.

But there was more that I wanted. I already had it. It was in the stands, somewhere behind home plate, where all the players' wives sat. In there was Lila, cheering for me just like I'd cheered for her when she won Olympic gold. Just like I would cheer for her in two more years when she joined the Olympic team again. Only things were slightly different now than they were a year ago during the Olympics. There were more reasons to cheer for one.

I made it to the mound, a crowd of players standing around it, each one giving me a high-five as I passed them. Players I had watched on television for years, admired and rooted for as my home team, accepting me as their peer. It gave me goosebumps.

I had to focus. This was the majors. I couldn't fuck it up. I took one look around the ballpark, letting myself soak it in for just a second. My name on the video board behind center right field sent electric shocks through my body. I felt like adrenaline was pumping through me harder than it ever had. I was getting tunnel vision. I needed to breathe.

I looked down the first base side to where Lila would be sitting. There they were. Kevin, Emma, Star, Mom, Lila... and Tiana. Our daughter. Lila stood, holding our baby up and showing off her adorable, cute pregnant belly. Baby number two was on the way. It was a good thing Kevin, Emma, and Star were so close. They loved being babysitters to their 'niece.' And Mom had shown herself to be a million times a better grandmother than she had been a mom.

The tight T-shirt pulled over Lila's belly had our faces on it. It was so cute I almost distracted myself from my mission. Her belly pushed the shirt out in a balloon shape. She was about ready to pop and was excited to do so. It would mean getting back on the field and returning to her spot on the national team, a spot that was safe after her MVP performance in the Olympics.

Our schedule with Tiana was already crazy. With me in the majors and her training for the Olympics, it was only going to get more hectic. But we would make it. We always did. We always would.

I bent over to stretch, thinking about what life would be like in a few years. When I was established as a major leaguer, a millionaire, and had months off in the winter to teach my own little boy and girl how to catch. It was going to be insane.

Lila and I wouldn't have it any other way.

She blew me a kiss as I looked back one last time, and I grinned. I threw my warm-up pitches and felt solid. Hot. Loose. I was ready to mow some motherfuckers down. This is what I was born for.

Mikie stood and signaled to the infield and the umpire called for the hitter to take his spot in the batter's box. I barely even noticed him. My focus was on the zone. The fingers of the catcher as he signed the complicated signal to tell me to throw a heater, high and tight, and then put his glove in the position he wanted it to go.

I grinned and stood.

I dug my foot down into the mound, the back part of my cleat pushing into the rubber. The umpire bent down over the catcher. The batter got set after his practice swing. I slid my fingers over the ball in my glove to find the right positions. Two fingers over the top seam, the thumb under the bottom. Four-seam fastball. *Here we go.*

I rocked back in my windup, my leg kick high like a Rockette. Then I shot forward, stretching as far down the mound as I could before I planted my left foot. My arm bent behind me as my chest led the way. I was going to give this one everything I had. Triple digits on the gun or bust.

It came off my fingers like lightning. Spinning tight and fast, cutting on a vertical line in toward the left-hand hitter. He took his step to swing, and the bat flew through the zone.

And missed.

"STRIKE!" the umpire called.

I looked over at Lila.

She was cheering. So was everyone. I smiled, knowing I had already won.

THE END

The Wrong Side of the Tracks

The Knockback
The Overshare
The Fightback

Find Lexy Timms:

Lexy Timms Newsletter:
http://www.lexytimms.com/newsletter
Lexy Timms Facebook Page:
https://www.facebook.com/LexyTimmsAuthor
Lexy Timms Website:
http://www.lexytimms.com

Lexy Timms
BOSS
Book 3
BOSS
Book 2
BOSS
Book 1
Managing BOSSES
Books 1-3
Lexy Timms
FREE
for a
Limited
Time

Want

FREE READS?

Sign up for Lexy Timms' newsletter
And she'll send you updates on new releases,
ARC copies of books and a whole lotta fun!

Sign up for news and updates!
http://www.lexytimms.com/newsletter

More by Lexy Timms:

FROM BEST SELLING AUTHOR, Lexy Timms, comes a billionaire romance that'll make you swoon and fall in love all over again.

Jamie Connors has given up on men. Despite being smart, pretty, and just slightly overweight, she's a magnet for the kind of guys that don't stay around.

Her sister's wedding is at the foreground of the family's attention. Jamie would be fine with it if her sister wasn't pressuring her to lose weight so she'll fit in the maid of honor dress, her mother would get off her case and her ex-boyfriend wasn't about to become her brother-in-law.

Determined to step out on her own, she accepts a PA position from billionaire Alex Reid. The job includes an apartment on his property and gets her out of living in her parent's basement.

Jamie must balance her life and somehow figure out how to manage her billionaire boss, without falling in love with him.

** The Boss is book 1 in the Managing the Bosses series. All your questions won't be answered in the first book. It may end on a cliff hanger.

For mature audiences only. There are adult situations, but this is a love story, NOT erotica.

THE ONE YOU CAN'T FORGET

Emily Rose Dougherty is a good Catholic girl from mythical Walkerville, CT. She had somehow managed to get herself into a heap trouble with the law, all because an ex-boyfriend has decided to make things difficult.

Luke "Spade" Wade owns a Motorcycle repair shop and is the Road Captain for Hades' Spawn MC. He's shocked when he reads in the paper that his old high school flame has been arrested. She's always been the one he couldn't forget.

Will destiny let them find each other again? Or what happens in the past, best left for the history books?

** *This is book 1 of the Hades' Spawn MC Series. All your questions may not be answered in the first book.*

A Burning Love Series

Book 1 – Spark of Passion

Book 2 – Flame of Desire

Book 3 – Blaze of Ecstasy

A Maybe Series

Book 1 – Maybe I Should
Book 2 – Maybe I Shouldn't
Book 3 – Maybe I Did

Don't miss out!

Visit the website below and you can sign up to receive emails whenever Lexy Timms publishes a new book. There's no charge and no obligation.

https://books2read.com/r/B-A-NNL-WVEAC

BOOKS 2 READ

Connecting independent readers to independent writers.

Did you love *The Fightback*? Then you should read *Troubled Nate Thomas - Part 1*[1] by Lexy Timms!

[2]

Bestselling romance author, Lexy Timms, brings you a new sport romance series that'll blow your mind—it's dynamite!

"TNT" – Troubled Nate Thomas...

Dubbed so by the media because Nate's always getting into trouble. Talented, handsome, and halfway out the door, Nate Thomas is on his last chance with the Denver Broncos. No one will deny he's got skills—on the field and in the bedroom. However, his taste for the party lifestyle, his drinking, and his anger issues are putting his career in jeopardy.

Coach Johnson wants his starting quarterback to actually play the way his big-money contract states he can. He needs to find a way to get

1. https://books2read.com/u/bP1LyR
2. https://books2read.com/u/bP1LyR

Nate's head back in the game. Threats, fines, and tickets don't seem to even slow Nate down.

With no choice but to try and risk the impossible, Coach Johnson hires a babysitter to look after Nate.

Amanda Jones is desperate for a job to help pay for her final year of her Master's. She's got a thesis to write and thinks being an au pair is the easiest way to get her work done, while making good money. She's stunned when she finds out she'll be taking care the infamous trouble-maker, Nate Thomas, aka TNT.

The money's too good to say no to, but can she somehow convince this train-wreck of an athlete to get his crap together before they both destroy the one thing they're good at?

Read more at www.lexytimms.com.

Also by Lexy Timms

12 Days of Christmas
Snowflake Hollow - Part 1
Snowflake Hollow - Part 2
Snowflake Hollow - Part 3
Snowflake Hollow - Part 4
Snowflake Hollow - Part 5
Snowflake Hollow - Part 6
Snowflake Hollow - Part 7
Snowflake Hollow - Part 8
Snowflake Hollow - Part 9
Snowflake Hollow - Part 10
Snowflake Hollow - Part 11
Snowflake Hollow - Part 12
Snowflake Hollow - Complete Series

A Bad Boy Bullied Romance
I Hate You
I Hate You A Little Bit
I Hate You A Little Bit More

A Bump in the Road Series
Expecting Love
Selfless Act
Doctor's Orders

A Burning Love Series
Spark of Passion
Flame of Desire
Blaze of Ecstasy

A Chance at Forever Series
Forever Perfect
Forever Desired
Forever Together

A Dark Casino Romance Series
High Roller
Place Your Bet
All Or Nothing

A Dark Mafia Romance Series
Taken By The Mob Boss
Truce With The Mob Boss
Taking Over the Mob Boss

Trouble For The Mob Boss
Tailored By The Mob Boss
Tricking the Mob Boss

A Dating App Series
I've Been Matched
You've Been Matched
We've Been Matched

A "Kind of" Billionaire
Taking a Risk
Safety in Numbers
Pretend You're Mine

A Maybe Series
Maybe I Should
Maybe I Shouldn't
Maybe I Did

A Royal Affair Series
Royally F*cked
Royally Screwed
Royally Obsessed

Assisting the Boss Series

Billion Reasons
Duke of Delegation
Late Night Meetings
Delegating Love
Suitors and Admirers

BBW Romance Series
Capturing Her Beauty
Pursuing Her Dreams
Tracing Her Curves

Beating the Biker Series
Making Her His
Making the Break
Making of Them

Betrayal at the Bay Series
Devil's Bay
Devil's Deceit
Devil's Duplicity

Billionaire Banker Series
Banking on Him
Price of Passion
Investing in Love
Knowing Your Worth

Treasured Forever
Banking on Christmas
Billionaire Banker Box Set Books #1-3

Billionaire CEO Brothers
Tempting the Player
Late Night Boardroom
Reviewing the Perfomance
Result of Passion
Directing the Next Move
Touching the Assets

Billionaire Hitman Series
The Hit
The Job
The Run

Billionaire Holiday Romance Series
Driving Home for Christmas
The Valentine Getaway
Cruising Love
Billionaire Holiday Romance Box Set

Billionaire in Disguise Series
Facade
Illusion

Charade

Billionaire Secrets Series

The Secret

Freedom

Courage

Trust

Impulse

Billionaire Secrets Box Set Books #1-3

Blind Sight Series

See Me

Fix Me

Eyes On Me

Branded Series

Money or Nothing

What People Say

Give and Take

Building Billions

Building Billions - Part 1

Building Billions - Part 2

Building Billions - Part 3

Butler & Heiress Series

To Serve

For Duty

No Chore

All Wrapped Up

Change of Heart Series

The Heart Needs

The Heart Wants

The Heart Knows

Club Confession Series

Envy

Crave

Decoy

Urge

Oath

Club Confession Box Set Books #1-3

Cottage by the Sea Series

Surging Tide

Distant Shores

Twisting Ocean

Counting the Billions
Counting the Days
Counting On You
Counting the Kisses

Cry Wolf Reverse Harem Series
Beautiful & Wild
Misunderstood
Never Tamed

Darkest Night Series
Savage
Vicious
Brutal
Sinful
Fierce

Diamond in the Rough Anthology
Billionaire Rock
Billionaire Rock - part 2

Dirty Little Taboo Series
Flirting Touch
Denying Pleasure

Forbidding Desire
Craving Passion

Dominating PA Series
Her Personal Assistant - Part 1
Her Personal Assistant - Part 2
Her Personal Assistant Box Set

Fake Billionaire Series
Faking It
Temporary CEO
Caught in the Act
Never Tell A Lie
Fake Christmas
Fake Billionaire Box Set #1-3

Firehouse Romance Series
Caught in Flames
Burning With Desire
Craving the Heat
Firehouse Romance Complete Collection

Forging Billions Series
Dirty Money
Petty Cash
Payment Required

For His Pleasure

Elizabeth

Georgia

Madison

Fortune Riders MC Series

Billionaire Biker

Billionaire Ransom

Billionaire Misery

Fortune Riders Box Set - Books #1-3

Fragile Series

Fragile Touch

Fragile Kiss

Fragile Love

Great Temptation Series

The Devil's Footsteps

Heaven's Command

Mortals Surrender

Hades' Spawn Motorcycle Club

One You Can't Forget

One That Got Away

One That Came Back
One You Never Leave
One Christmas Night
Hades' Spawn MC Complete Series

Hard Rocked Series
Rhyme
Harmony
Lyrics

Heart of Stone Series
The Protector
The Guardian
The Warrior

Heart of the Battle Series
Celtic Viking
Celtic Rune
Celtic Mann
Heart of the Battle Series Box Set

Heistdom Series
Master Thief
Goldmine
Diamond Heist
Smile For Me

Your Move
Green With Envy
Saving Money

Highlander Wolf Series
Pack Run
Pack Land
Pack Rules

Hollyweird Fae Series
Inception of Gold
Disruption of Magic
Guardians of Twilight

How To Love A Spy
The Secret
The Secret Life
The Secret Wife

Just About Series
About Love
About Truth
About Forever
Just About Box Set Books #1-3

Justice Series
Seeking Justice
Finding Justice
Chasing Justice
Pursuing Justice
Justice - Complete Series

Karma Series
Walk Away
Make Him Pay
Perfect Revenge

King of Hades MC Series
Sinner
Tempting Sinner
Enticing Sinner

Kissed by Billions
Kissed by Passion
Kissed by Desire
Kissed by Love

Leaning Towards Trouble
Trouble

Discord
Tenacity

Love on the Sea Series
Ships Ahoy
Rough Sea
High Tide

Lovers in London Series
Risking Millions
Venture Capital
Worth the Expense
The Price of Luxury
Exclusive Passion
Sparkling Christmas
Lovers in London - 3 Book Box Set

Love You Series
Love Life
Need Love
My Love

Managing the Billionaire
Never Enough
Worth the Cost
Secret Admirers

Chasing Affection
Pressing Romance
Timeless Memories
Managing the Billionaire Box Set Books #1-3

Managing the Bosses Series
The Boss
The Boss Too
Who's the Boss Now
Love the Boss
I Do the Boss
Wife to the Boss
Employed by the Boss
Brother to the Boss
Senior Advisor to the Boss
Forever the Boss
Christmas With the Boss
Billionaire in Control
Billionaire Makes Millions
Billionaire at Work
Precious Little Thing
Priceless Love
Valentine Love
The Cost of Freedom
Trick or Treat
The Night Before Christmas
Gift for the Boss - Novella 3.5
Managing the Bosses Box Set #1-3
Managing the Bosses Novellas

Mislead by the Bad Boy Series

Deceived

Provoked

Betrayed

Model Mayhem Series

Shameless

Modesty

Imperfection

Moment in Time

Highlander's Bride

Victorian Bride

Modern Day Bride

A Royal Bride

Forever the Bride

Mountain Millionaire Series

Close to the Ridge

Crossing the Bluff

Climbing the Mount

My Best Friend's Sister

Hometown Calling

A Perfect Moment
Thrown in Together

My Darker Side Series
Darkest Hour
Time to Stop
Against the Light

Neverending Dream Series
Neverending Dream - Part 1
Neverending Dream - Part 2
Neverending Dream - Part 3
Neverending Dream - Part 4
Neverending Dream - Part 5
Neverending Dream Box Set Books #1-3

Outside the Octagon
Submit
Fight
Knockout

Protecting Diana Series
Her Bodyguard
Her Defender
Her Champion
Her Protector

Her Forever
Protecting Diana Box Set Books #1-3

Protecting Layla Series
His Mission
His Objective
His Devotion

Racing Hearts Series
Rush
Pace
Fast

Regency Romance Series
The Duchess Scandal - Part 1
The Duchess Scandal - Part 2

Reverse Harem Series
Primals
Archaic
Unitary

Roommate Wanted Series
The Roommate
The Bunkmate

The Flatmate

R&S Rich and Single Series

Alex Reid

Parker

Sebastian

Zane

Saving Forever

Saving Forever - Part 1

Saving Forever - Part 2

Saving Forever - Part 3

Saving Forever - Part 4

Saving Forever - Part 5

Saving Forever - Part 6

Saving Forever Part 7

Saving Forever - Part 8

Saving Forever Boxset Books #1-3

Secrets & Lies Series

Strange Secrets

Evading Secrets

Inspiring Secrets

Lies and Secrets

Mastering Secrets

Alluring Secrets

Secrets & Lies Box Set Books #1-3

Shifting Desires Series

Jungle Heat

Jungle Fever

Jungle Blaze

Sin Series

Payment for Sin

Atonement Within

Declaration of Love

Southern Romance Series

Little Love Affair

Siege of the Heart

Freedom Forever

Soldier's Fortune

Spanked Series

Passion

Playmate

Pleasure

Spelling Love Series

The Author

The Book Boyfriend

The Words of Love

Strength & Style

Suits You, Sir

Tailor Made

Perfect Gentleman

Taboo Wedding Series

He Loves Me Not

With This Ring

Happily Ever After

Tattooist Series

Confession of a Tattooist

Surrender of a Tattooist

Heart of a Tattooist

Hopes & Dreams of a Tattooist

Tennessee Romance

Whisky Lullaby

Whisky Melody

Whisky Harmony

The Bad Boy Alpha Club

Battle Lines - Part 1

Battle Lines

The Brush Of Love Series
Every Night
Every Day
Every Time
Every Way
Every Touch
The Brush of Love Series Box Set Books #1-3

The City of Mayhem Series
True Mayhem
Relentless Chaos
Broken Disorder

The Debt
The Debt: Part 1 - Damn Horse
The Debt: Complete Collection

The Fire Inside Series
Dare Me
Defy Me
Burn Me

The Gentleman's Club Series

Gambler
Player
Wager

The Golden Game
On The Pitch
Respect the Game
All Game
Sweat and Tears
The Final Score
The Golden Game Box Set Books #1-3

The Golden Mail
Hot Off the Press
Extra! Extra!
Read All About It
Stop the Press
Breaking News
This Just In
The Golden Mail Box Set Books #1-3

The Long Con Series
The Misfit
The Hustle

The Lucky Billionaire Series

Lucky Break
Streak of Luck
Lucky in Love

The Millionaire's Pretty Woman Series
Perfect Stranger
Captive Devotion
Sweet Temptations

The Sound of Breaking Hearts Series
Disruption
Destroy
Devoted

The University of Gatica Series
The Recruiting Trip
Faster
Higher
Stronger
Dominate
No Rush
University of Gatica - The Complete Series

The Wrong Side of the Tracks
The Knockback
The Overshare

The Fightback

Timing is Everything Series
Right Time
Right Place
Right Reasons

T.N.T. Series
Troubled Nate Thomas - Part 1
Troubled Nate Thomas - Part 2
Troubled Nate Thomas - Part 3

Toxic Touch Series
Noxious
Lethal
Willful
Tainted
Craved
Toxic Touch Box Set Books #1-3

Undercover Boss Series
Marketing
Finance
Legal

Undercover Series

Perfect For Me

Perfect For You

Perfect For Us

Unknown Identity Series

Unknown

Unpublished

Unexposed

Unsure

Unwritten

Unknown Identity Box Set: Books #1-3

Unlucky Series

Unlucky in Love

UnWanted

UnLoved Forever

War Torn Letters Series

My Sweetheart

My Darling

My Beloved

Wet & Wild Series

Stormy Love
Savage Love
Secure Love

Worth It Series
Worth Billions
Worth Every Cent
Worth More Than Money

You & Me - A Bad Boy Romance
Just Me
Touch Me
Kiss Me

Standalone
Wash
Loving Charity
Summer Lovin'
Love & College
Billionaire Heart
First Love
Frisky and Fun Romance Box Collection
Beating Hades' Bikers
Everyone Loves a Bad Boy
Dead of Night

Watch for more at www.lexytimms.com.

About the Author

"Love should be something that lasts forever, not is lost forever." Visit USA TODAY BESTSELLING AUTHOR, LEXY TIMMS https://www.facebook.com/SavingForever *Please feel free to connect with me and share your comments. I love connecting with my readers.* Sign up for news and updates and freebies - I like spoiling my readers! http://eepurl.com/9i0vD website: www.lexytimms.com Dealing in Antique Jewelry and hanging out with her awesome hubby and three kids, Lexy Timms loves writing in her free time. MANAGING THE BOSSES is a bestselling 10-part series dipping into the lives of Alex Reid and Jamie Connors. Can a secretary really fall for her billionaire boss?

Read more at www.lexytimms.com.